# Let Sleeping Hedgehogs Spy

## By Elizabeth Morley

Published in 2013 by FeedARead.com Publishing – Arts Council funded

First Edition

A CIP catalogue record for this title is available from the British Library.

For Lavinia and Edward

# Prologue

Far off up the mountain were three tiny pinpricks of light - the torches of the hedgehogs who were after him. Snipper felt the miniature spy camera in his pocket to reassure himself it was still there. It was. Shielding his own torch with his paw, he checked his map. There was a fork coming up. If he skied left, this would take him through the trees, where he had the best chance of losing his pursuers. He put away his map and torch and examined the snowy slope below him: there was the fork not far ahead and just beyond it the wood. Leaning forward on his skis, he pushed off.

Snipper slipped down the mountain at high speed, slowing very slightly as he plunged into the darkness of the wood. Now he had only the feel of the ground beneath his skis and the occasional glint of moonlight between the trees to guide him; but he was trained for this sort of thing and was an expert skier by day and by night. As he skied through the woods, there was no sign of his pursuers. Save for the swish of his own skis, there was complete silence. Re-emerging from the trees, he saw the twinkle of village lights in the valley far below. The village meant safety. He thought of the hedgehogs there, safe and snug in front of their log fires.

"There he is!" shouted a voice far too close for comfort. Snipper turned his head and saw the outline of a hedgehog silhouetted against the snow. How on earth...?

There was no time to think - no time to wonder how they had caught up with him so suddenly. He pushed hard on his poles and directed his skis straight down the fall line. But soon the swoosh of the pursuing hedgehogs could be heard clearly behind him. Then there was a click - the sound of a gun's safety catch being released. *Rat-tat-tat!* A burst of bullets whizzed past him as his pursuers opened fire. One grazed his arm but he skied on regardless. He pushed on and on down the mountain, through more trees and then out into the clear until, suddenly, the piste vanished from beneath him. He was falling, clawing the air as he fell, plummeting into the void -

Snipper woke with a start, the fur on his face matted with sweat and his heart thumping. He was safe in bed, at home in his cosy little flat. There were no enemy hedgehogs pursuing him and no cliffs over which he could fall. He smiled at his foolishness but then frowned: he had never dreamed about work before.

He wondered why he did so now. He had worked as a secret agent for the last four years but it had never affected his sleep before. He might have expected to dream about his imminent skiing holiday, which he was very much looking forward to. But somehow the skiing and the spying had got all mixed up together.

Sitting up in bed, he decided that the stress of working alone under deep cover must be finally getting to him. He had never told either his friends or his family what he really did for a living: they believed him to be an art dealer. It was the perfect cover - it explained why he worked alone from home and why he travelled so much. In reality, though, he belonged to an élite wing of the Bristlish Secret Service: the Special Licence Undercover Group - known as S.L.U.G. for short. It was not only a dangerous job but a lonely one, too. S.L.U.G. agents worked on their own. Their special licence allowed them to make instant decisions in the field without having to get the approval of a more senior officer. Unlike ordinary secret agents, they never went to Secret Service H.Q. but communicated via a secure computer network. Direct contact with colleagues was usually limited to the occasional clandestine meeting on a park bench or in some dingy café.

Snipper sighed. He would have liked to have someone with whom he could share his secret - with whom he could talk; but it was simply too dangerous and his job would always have to come first. He slipped out of bed and into his dressing gown, and shuffled into the kitchen to make himself some coffee. He was tired - very tired.

For the next few days, however, there would be no spying and no assassins lurking in the shadows. Even secret agents take holidays from time to time: Snipper was about to have his.

# Part One
## Chapter One

Snipper had been invited to visit his friend, Thistley, at her home in Clawtina, a beautiful ski resort in the mountains of northern Itchaly. The two hedgehogs were close friends and, though Thistley had moved overseas, they still managed to see each other several times a year. This visit was to be a special one, though, for their friends Pawline and Scratch were coming, too. All four hedgehogs had been at university together in Great Bristlin; but Pawline had gone back home to the United Stakes soon afterwards, and it was a very long time since they had all been together.

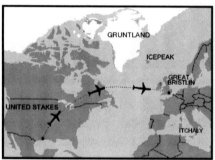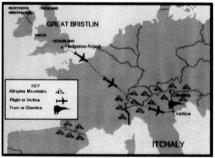

It was therefore with some excitement that Snipper packed his bags. Of course, he took no time at all to choose his clothes and gather together his skiing gear - as a secret agent, he spent half his life living out of a suitcase and could pack with his eyes shut. But he did pause over his paints. He was uncertain whether to take oils or watercolours. Oils were easier to paint with but watercolours were less messy and more portable... He hummed and hawed until eventually his thoughts were interrupted by his telephone beeping. It was a message from Major Dirkby, his boss, telling him to read a report which had just come in. Snipper looked at his watch and sighed. He had fifteen minutes to spare but then he would have to leave pretty sharpish if he was going to catch his flight. He went out into the hall, lifted a picture off the wall - uncovering the key pad hidden behind it - and tapped in his secret code. A moment later there was a whirring sound, then the rosette on the hall ceiling lifted back into the roof space above and a ladder started to descend. He waited for the ladder to reach the floor and then climbed up into his secret office.

Downstairs, Snipper had a study full of papers relating to antiquities, auction houses, museums and private collectors. However, that existed only to support his cover as an art dealer. Here, in the attic, was his real office - the place where he planned his secret operations and communicated with Secret Service H.Q.. It was where he stored the disguises and false documents which allowed him to assume different identities. He also kept all kinds of secret agent gadgets up here - from listening bugs and false-bottomed briefcases to tiny cameras disguised as almost anything you could think of.

Sitting down at his computer, Snipper typed in his password and presented his right paw to the scanner, which then compared it with the pawprint in its files. He waited a few seconds until the words "Access Granted" flashed up on the screen: he was in. The report Dirkby wanted him to look at was about a hedgehog from the Needlelands called Van Hogloot. Van Hogloot was believed to act as unofficial banker to the criminal classes, and Dirkby wanted to know whether Snipper had come across him before. The report made surprisingly interesting reading. In a list of the hedgehogs Van Hogloot had recently been in contact with were the names of four of the biggest criminal masterminds in the world. Clearly something was afoot, though there did not seem to be much urgency about it. Snipper typed a brief message saying, yes, he had come across Van

Hogloot a couple of years ago - when he had been investigating a case of diamond smuggling. He attached the file from the investigation and pressed *send*. Then he glanced anxiously at his watch. It was 10.55, and he should have left a full five minutes ago. He hastily closed up his office, threw both his watercolours and his oils into his suitcase and left.

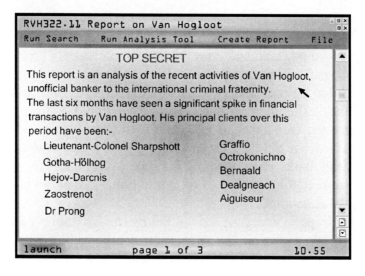

## Chapter Two

Snipper and his friends landed in Itchaly as darkness fell and took a water taxi to Vertice, where they were to spend their first night - before catching the snow train to Clawtina the following morning. Vertice was a beautiful old city built on a cluster of islands and famous for its countless canals and bridges. Furthermore, its winter carnival was in full swing, and Pawline was anxious to get a taste of it.

When they arrived, they found the streets bristling with hedgehogs - all wearing fancy dress and masks for the carnival. Scratch led Snipper and Pawline down a series of narrow alleyways until they came to their hotel, the *Ca' di Punto*. Going straight to their rooms, they changed into their own fancy dress costumes and masks. Snipper put on a green velvet jacket, a pair of dark breeches and white mask. Then, slinging his cape over his arm, he proceeded downstairs to join his friends for a traditional cup of hot chocolate in the hotel restaurant.

Like Snipper, everyone else in the room was wearing fancy dress and a mask. However, he soon spotted a hedgehog with Scratch's build seated by himself at a window table. He went over.

"Hallo - it's me," he said, taking a seat. The other hedgehog looked at him in puzzled silence. "Come on, Scratch, I *know* it's you!" he persisted, even prodding him with a claw.

"Oh, all right then!" laughed Scratch. "Just having a bit of fun!... Hey, isn't that Pawline coming downstairs? She said she'd be wearing a long purple dress." He waved a paw. "Over here, Pawline!"

The hedgehog in the purple dress hesitated for a moment and then waved back.

"You look great," said Scratch approvingly as she joined them.

"Gee, thanks!" she responded in the distinct accent of the United Stakes. "I'm glad you like it - I took an age choosing it... But you and Snipper look pretty cute in your outfits, too. So, anyway, what do you recommend?"

"I think hot chocolate's meant to be the order of the day," said Scratch, picking up his menu. "Oh, and this looks interesting - *Frittelle di Carnivale.* Do you know what that is, Snipper?"

"Local doughnuts. It's traditional to eat them during the carnival - hence the name."

"Cool! I reckon we should get some of those," said Pawline enthusiastically. Then she looked at Snipper quizzically. "Hey, Snipper, are there any languages you *don't* speak?"

"Plenty," he said modestly.

"Kinda funny really. Your being so smart and so scatter-brained all at once."

"Am I?" said Snipper, who was a little surprised to be called scatter-brained.

"Yeah, sure you are, so don't be so prickly about it! I mean, like today - you were cutting it real fine getting the flight. You're always late for things."

"Snipper just likes to live life on the edge!" joked Scratch.

"As it happens, I had an important deal I had to wrap up before I left," lied Snipper. "I was buying an ancient and extremely rare Tippuyu pot for a very important client in Hogotà."

"You don't say!" responded Pawline, who had no idea what a Tippuyu pot was but was trying hard to be interested.

"So the old pots and pans are keeping you busy then?" said Scratch.

"Pretty much," said Snipper. "What about you two? Been up to anything lately?" Snipper was hoping to deflect the conversation. It usually worked, because neither Pawline nor Scratch was really interested in old pots, however hard they tried to be. What was more, both of them led action-packed lives of their own. Scratch was an officer in the Royal Engineers of the Bristlish army, which meant he was forever travelling to interesting places. Meanwhile, Pawline was a trainee astronaut. After two years of training, she was waiting to have her selection confirmed.

"Actually, I've got some big news!" said Pawline, as bright as a new pin.

"Don't tell me you've finally heard from the selection board?" said Snipper.

"I sure have!" confirmed Pawline, beaming.

"Well, that's fantastic!" said Scratch. He did not have to be told the result: the expression on her face said it all.

"Yeah, and they're sending me to the International Space Station."

*"Prego, signori?"* It was the waiter, who had come to take their order.

*"Tre cioccolate calde, un piatto di frittelle e una bottiglia di prosecco, per favore,"* said Snipper, ordering three hot chocolates, a plate of doughnuts and a bottle of sparkling wine.

"Prosecco - that's the local champagne, isn't it?" said Scratch. "What an excellent idea! We've definitely got some celebrating to do."

The waiter disappeared off into the kitchen, and the three friends turned their attention to Scratch's news. Since they had last seen him, he had been to Icepeak, an extraordinary island of volcanoes and ice which lay in the middle of the ocean, halfway between the United Stakes and Great Bristlin. Scratch had gone there on exercise with the hedgehogs under his command.

"Well," said Scratch, "we parachuted into the wilderness and then had to make our way to the sea on foot. It was hard work - with mile upon mile of black volcanic sand and not a hedgehog in sight. When we finally made it out of the wilderness, we really appreciated the sight of green grass, I can tell you! And the waterfall at Gatafoss - you know, that spectacular one, which all the tourists visit - well, that just knocked us for six. Only annoying thing is I think I dropped my hip flask there - you know, the one my parents gave me. That aside, though, it was a good trip. I've printed off a few photographs if you'd like to see them."

Snipper took the photographs and looked through them with Pawline. "What's that?," he asked, pointing to a strange grey shape in the background of one. It looked like some sort of ironwork tower.

"I don't know," responded Scratch. "It wasn't marked on our maps but I suppose it could be a mobile phone mast."

"Out in the wilderness?"

Scratch shrugged his shoulders, and the waiter appeared with their order. So the three friends tucked into the doughnuts and hot chocolate, while Scratch described how they had made it out of Icepeak's wilderness. Then the subject changed to Pawline's forthcoming mission to the International Space Station. Opening the wine, they drank a toast to her selection and chatted at length about the experiments she would be carrying out on board the station. They then even talked about Tippuyu pottery for a bit, though on the whole Snipper was happy to let his friends hog the conversation. Eventually, of course, the talk turned to the holiday itself. Pawline was clearly very excited about seeing Thistley again after such a long time. Scratch said he was looking forward to doing some climbing as well as skiing, having read that Clawtina was a good place for it.

15

Snipper, however, had stopped listening, distracted by the sound of music coming from the piazza outside. Gazing out of the window, he watched the musicians - buskers collecting money for charity by the look of it.

"Hey! How about that!" said Pawline, following Snipper's gaze. "Isn't that a mandolin? Don't you reckon, Snipper?"

"Yes, I think you're right," agreed Snipper. There were three of them: a violinist, a flautist and the mandolin player - all in masks and fancy dress. They were, indeed, very good. "Why don't we go out and listen to them properly?" suggested Snipper, who felt strangely drawn to the music.

"Can't see the point," said Scratch. "It'll be freezing standing around out there in these clothes. In any case we're already going to a concert later tonight."

"You've got no sense of romance," said Pawline. "Street music is completely different than a formal concert."

"If you say so..." said Scratch doubtfully. "Look, why don't you two go on ahead? I'll pay the bill and join you in five."

Snipper and Pawline put on their cloaks, then went outside and crossed the bridge to the little piazza where the buskers were playing. Behind the buskers hung a home-made banner with "Vertice in peril!" written upon it in Itchalian. They were collecting money to help save the city. It was certainly an expensive cause: the city was a treasure trove of art and architecture built on an island of soft sand and mud; gradually, year after year, it was sinking into the sea and it was going to cost a lot to stop that. But it was a good cause, too, and, judging by the collection box, Snipper was not the only one who thought so.

Snipper glanced round the piazza at the other hedgehogs in the crowd. As elsewhere, they were dressed in fancy costumes and masks; but there was something particularly magical about this place. Standing beneath the flickering gaslight, with the moonlight glistening in the canal below and music playing all the while, Snipper and Pawline felt themselves transported to another time.

When the piece came to an end, the mandolin player addressed the audience: *"Grazie mille!"* she said, as the applause died away. *"Sono molto contenta che la mia composizione vi è piaciuto."*

Snipper was impressed. Apparently, the piece of music which had drawn them out into the piazza was her own composition. He joined in the enthusiastic applause, until she held up a paw for silence and announced that they would now be playing a piece by the famous baroque composer, Albospinoni. Picking up her mandolin, she made eye contact with her fellow players. Then the music started again.

It was an attractive piece but Snipper rather wished she had gone

on speaking, for her voice had a mesmerizing musical quality all of its own. He wondered if it was just the accent. Happily for the buskers, the choice of music proved popular and gradually the crowd got bigger until it was quite a squash in the little piazza. A succession of hedgehogs came forward to put money in the collection box. One - a hedgehog in a black cape, tricorne hat and mask - pushed his way to the front, placed a pawful of notes in the box and then left without stopping to listen. Snipper watched this and could have sworn the stranger had taken an envelope out of the box while putting the money in. When he turned round his paws were empty - but an envelope can easily be tucked up a sleeve. There was, in any case, something distinctly odd about giving a large donation and then not even stopping to listen.

Snipper had a nose for trouble and an instinct to follow his nose. Without a word to Pawline, he pushed his way back through the crowd and scanned the quayside looking for the masked stranger. For a moment it looked as though he had lost him but then he spotted the black cape and tricorne hat: the stranger was crossing the footbridge towards the *Hotel Ca' di Punto.* Snipper followed at a distance. As he reached the far side of the bridge, the stranger disappeared down a dark alleyway, his footsteps echoing loudly in the confined space. Snipper paused to take off his own shoes.

"There you are, Snipper!" came Pawline's voice suddenly beside him. "What on earth were you doing, wandering off like that?" The stranger spun round, and Snipper caught a glimpse of something in his paw - it looked like a gun but he could not be sure. Not seeing any of this, Pawline stepped straight into the line of sight. The stranger immediately withdrew into the shadows. Snipper turned to Pawline and smiled weakly. It was useless trying to follow.

The following morning Snipper, Scratch and Pawline took the water taxi to the railway station for the last leg of their journey to Clawtina. Being in good time, they walked to the train in a leisurely fashion. Pawline stopped at a kiosk to buy herself a tall half-skinny decaff latte. While she queued and Scratch checked his emails, Snipper idly surveyed the scene. Just in front of Pawline, a hoglet was tugging at his mother's sleeve, trying to attract her attention. Next in line was an elderly hedgehog rubbing her paws together to keep warm. At the head of the queue, a sharp-suited hedgehog was stretching out his paw to receive his change. As he did so, the sleeve of his jacket pulled back to reveal a monogrammed cufflink. Snipper recognized the monogram at once. It belonged to none other than Mr E, an infamous criminal genius, whose identity was a mystery no one was able to solve. No hedgehog on the right side of the law had ever laid eyes on Mr E before. Indeed, such was the secrecy and security surrounding him that few hedgehogs on the wrong side of the law had seen him either. His monogram, however, was known to Snipper, as it appeared on all his communications.

The sharp-suited hedgehog picked up his caffè normale and proceeded down the platform to the snow train. Slipping away from

his friends, Snipper followed him onto the train. He paused in the doorway while his hedgehog found his seat. Then he entered the carriage and committed his face to memory as he walked past. There was something rather nondescript about that face, and Snipper suspected he could pass unnoticed almost anywhere. Today he might be a hedgehog-about-town but tomorrow he could just as easily pass for a factory worker or bank clerk. Fortunately, Snipper had a very good memory for faces.

Just behind and across the gangway from Mr E was an empty seat. Snipper took it and, watching him, reflected on the vanity that led him to wear monogrammed cufflinks; vanity was a failing Snipper had often observed in criminals who made it big. Of course, this could just be one of Mr E's minions wearing his master's badge. But Snipper felt sure it was Mr E, himself. He had a nose for such things, and this hedgehog had an air of authority about him.

Next Snipper fell to examining the hedgehogs sitting opposite Mr E. The window seat was occupied by an elderly hedgehog slumped in a deep sleep. Next to him was a hedgehog about the same age as Snipper. She wore a pale blue dress and gold necklace. Judging by her elegance, Snipper guessed she must be a native of Itchaly. He watched her in a slightly distracted sort of way until the book on her lap fell to the floor, jolting him out of his trance.

Mr E bent over to pick up the book. *"Ecco qua!"* he said, returning it to its owner - and, then, glancing at its cover: *"Ah, 'Sei Ericii in Cerca di un Autore'! È molto affascinante, vero?"*

Snipper listened intently, trying to catch every word. It seemed that the book was "Six Hedgehogs in Search of an Author" - a well-known play, which Mr E said he found fascinating.

*"Si, ma è un po' difficile."* replied the hedgehog in the blue dress. Apparently she agreed with Mr E but found the play quite difficult.

Here the conversation ended. On the face of it, the hedgehog in blue was nothing to do with Mr E. She was just a stranger whose book he had picked up off the floor for her. And Snipper would have paid no further attention to her - but for the fact that he had heard her voice before. In fact, he had no difficulty at all in pinning it down: she was the mandolin player from Vertice. He would have recognized her voice anywhere.

Snipper felt there had to be a connection between last night and now. The envelope in the collection box must have been a message for Mr E - probably the arrangements for this very meeting. The conversation about the book was perhaps some sort of password or code.

These thoughts were interrupted by the sight of Scratch boarding the next carriage. Snipper sprang up from his seat and hurried

towards the door. The last thing he wanted was to have his name shouted out again. The previous night both he and the stranger had been masked; but, now he had seen Mr E's face, he had the upper paw and he wanted it to stay that way. Scratch entered the carriage just as Snipper reached the doorway.

"So here you are, Snipper!" said Scratch, bristling with irritation. "You do know you're in the wrong carriage, don't you?"

Snipper sensed he was being watched but by now he had his back to Mr E and the hedgehog in blue, so his identity was safe. They had his name, to be sure, but that would not help them much. As a deep cover secret agent, he always worked under an alias - Snipper the art dealer was of interest to no one but his friends.

Snipper followed Scratch through the doorway, and they joined Pawline in the correct seats a couple of carriages along. He had some explaining to do, of course. This was the second time he had wandered off without a word, and his friends were beginning to find his behaviour a little tiresome. He apologized profusely, explaining that he had thought he had recognized an old schoolfriend.

Of course, this could hardly be the end of the matter. Snipper had an important lead to follow up. With his friends around, however, it was impossible for him to operate effectively. He would have to brief Dirkby and pass this one on. While the others were engaged in conversation, he got his phone out, tapped in his pin number and then waited while his paw was scanned. After a moment, the screen changed colour, showing Snipper that he was now in secure mode.

*Important lead,* he wrote. *Possible connection to your report. Cannot follow it up myself without breaking cover. Send best available agent to meet me on the Vertice-Clawtina train.*

Snipper glanced at his friends but they were paying no attention to him. So far as they were concerned, it was just an ordinary telephone and Snipper was sending an ordinary text. He selected Dirkby from his contacts, then pressed *send* and put away his phone. It would be a relief to be shot of this lead and able to concentrate on his friends and his holiday. But he could not help feeling a twinge of regret. Was it because this promised to be something big? Perhaps. On the other hand, for some reason, he could not get the hedgehog in the blue dress out of his head...

"Listen to this," said Pawline, who had her nose in a newspaper. "Further heavy snowfalls expected in the Altispine Mountains in Itchaly. Danger of avalanches."

"Does it mention Clawtina?" asked Scratch.

"No, it's too general for that. Tell you what, I'll check my cellphone - see if I can get any more details."

As Pawline surfed the web for further news, Snipper's own mobile beeped. It was an email from Pinmoney, Dirkby's assistant: *Agent 27 already in Itchaly at Lametta, your next stop. Will join train at Lametta wearing green coat & black trousers. Identify yourself with password: IT LOOKS PRETTY CHILLY OUT THERE. Response will be: YES, IT'S GOOD TO COME IN FROM THE COLD.*

Snipper breathed an inward sigh of relief. Dirkby was sending one of his very best S.L.U.G. agents: Pierce, known to his colleagues as Agent 27. Snipper had never met Pierce before but he knew him by reputation. He had been in the spying game for a long time, and it was said that no one did it better.

"Anything interesting?" asked Scratch. "It isn't Thistley warning us about avalanches, by any chance?"

"No, there's no news from Thistley," said Snipper. It was a pity, he thought to himself, that this rendezvous with Pierce could not take place a little sooner. He had no way of knowing how long Mr E and the hedgehog in blue would stay on the train now that they had met. He decided that a trip to the buffet car would give him the chance to check up on them. "Anyone want anything to eat or drink?" he asked, getting up from his seat.

He took his friends' orders and, removing his coat to avoid being recognized, went on his way. Mr E was still in his seat; the hedgehog in the blue dress was gone. However, Snipper pressed on to the buffet car and found her there. Somehow, he had to engage her in conversation. A tingle of excitement ran down his spines as he placed his order and observed her out of the corner of his eye. She certainly did not seem to be in any hurry. She took her time putting her change away and then started checking her phone for messages.

"Excuse me," said Snipper, addressing her in Hedgelandish. There was no need at this stage to admit he spoke Itchalian. Indeed, over the years, he had found out a great deal of useful information by pretending ignorance of other languages. "Are you from around here?"

"Yes - 'ow can I 'elp you?" she replied with a distinctly Itchalian accent.

24

"I was just wondering whether you knew anything about the risk of avalanches that's been reported in the news. My friends and I are going skiing in Clawtina and we're a bit worried. None of us knows the area."

"*Capita?* Risk of avalanges? I was not-a knowing. I also go to Clawtina. Let-a me see..." She checked her phone. "Yes, dere are several closèd pistes aroun' Tagliento and Setola; but Clawtina itself is OK."

"That's a relief - thank you," said Snipper. "So you're going to Clawtina, too? Perhaps I'll see you on the piste."

"I doubt - it is a very, very big area," she said with a shrug of the shoulders. It clearly meant nothing to her if she never saw him again. Why should it? "Well, it was nice to meet you, Mr...?"

"The name's Snipper - just Snipper."

" 'Ow do you do, Snipper?" She shook paws with him but then turned tail and left without giving him her own name. Snipper gazed after her as she disappeared into the next carriage.

What had he been thinking? She had not given him her name, so what on earth had induced him to give her his? After all the care he had taken to avoid being identified! Mr E had only to tell her he had been tailed by a hedgehog called Snipper (if he had not done so already), and Snipper's cover really was blown. They had seen his interest in them, they had his real name and now they knew what he looked like, too. He could not understand his own behaviour. Though modest by nature, he was well aware that he was one of the Bristlish Secret Service's top agents - simply because only the very best were asked to join S.L.U.G.. Now it was as though he had forgotten all his training. To be sure, the situation was hedged about with difficulties. Never before had his private and professional worlds collided like this. Having Pawline and Scratch with him meant he was stuck with using his real name; and, being on holiday, he had no alias documentation with him anyway. But he felt sure he could have handled the situation better.

Snipper was furious with himself. However, it was done now and there was no point dwelling on it. He picked up his order and made his way back down the train to rejoin his friends. The hedgehog in blue was back in her seat, opposite Mr E. Snipper smiled faintly as he passed her but said nothing. She appeared not to notice him at all, and he continued on his way without pausing.

"You've been gone a long time!" said Scratch, when Snipper got back to his own carriage. "We thought we'd lost you again! Was there a long queue?"

"No, I was just trying to find out about the avalanche risk. Apparently - " he started to explain; but then he was interrupted by an announcement over the loud speaker, first in Itchalian and then in Hedgelandish.

"Ladies and gentle'ogs, you are advisèd dat de train will terminate at de next-a station because of de risk of avalanges. We tank you for your patience..."

"I don't believe it!" groaned Pawline. "What do we do now?"

"There may be a bus we can take," said Scratch, "or, if not, we could always hire a car."

"Wouldn't it be sensible to wait and see what the advice is?" suggested Snipper. "The roads may be closed as well."

The roads were closed. On arriving at the next station, the passengers were booked into a hotel and told to wait for an update in the morning. It was very disappointing, especially for Pawline, who had flown all the way from the United Stakes for this holiday. For Snipper, however, there was one important advantage. On the train there had been no possibility of searching the luggage of Mr E or the hedgehog in blue; the hotel, on the other hand, offered the perfect opportunity. Snipper emailed Secret Service H.Q. with the latest news, while Pawline texted Thistley about the delay.

At the hotel, they were given three rooms on the fifth floor. They took their keys and made their way to the lift. Snipper got in with Pawline and Scratch but then jumped back out again. "Sorry - forgot to ask what time breakfast was!" he said, as though he had just thought of it. "I'll catch you up." The lift doors closed before either of his friends could speak.

Snipper now wandered back towards the reception desk where he lurked behind a potted bamboo, waiting for Mr E and the hedgehog in blue to check in. They approached the receptionist separately, as though travelling alone, but that proved nothing. They could be working together paw-in-glove but still not acknowledge one another in public. Snipper listened for their names and room numbers: Signorina Despina and Signor Pungolo, in 648 and 407, respectively. Then, as they walked away from the desk, he secretly photographed each of them with his mobile phone.

Snipper now returned to his friends but continued to keep an eye out for Mr E and Despina during the rest of the day. His opportunity came shortly after lunch, when he saw Despina give her key in at reception and leave the hotel. He waited a couple of minutes in case she came back having forgotten something. Then, as soon as the receptionist was looking away, he pushed over the potted bamboo and slipped out of sight round the corner. A moment later, there was an exclamation of dismay. Snipper reappeared to find the bamboo upright once more and the receptionist scooping up pawfuls of earth and placing it back in the pot.

Behind the desk, the key for room 648 now hung unattended. With a quick glance to ensure that the receptionist was still preoccupied by the bamboo, he simply took the key and went directly to Despina's room. When he arrived outside her door, he looked round to make sure there was no one else about, then he let himself in and locked the door behind him. He got to work immediately - searching the room thoroughly but quickly (for there was no telling when Despina might return to see that her key had been taken). All he found were some rather stylish clothes hanging up in the wardrobe, a small case of expensive-looking jewellery and the book which she had discussed with Mr E on the train. Snipper pawed through its pages, looking for signs that it had been used for secret communications - underlinings, scribbles in the margins, the corner of a page turned back or perhaps a postcard inserted between the pages. There were none; the book just looked well read.

Mr E's room was next and Snipper decided to go the whole hog this time. He wanted to search his wallet and mobile but, to have any real chance of getting hold of such personal items, he would have to conduct his search while Mr E was in his bathroom. It was high risk, of course, but Snipper had been trained to take risks.

When evening came, Snipper turned in early. Being on holiday, he had none of his special secret agent equipment with him; however, he did have his smartphone, a roll of sticky tape he had borrowed from reception, a candle he had pinched from the restaurant and the lid from his tin of drawing pencils. He put these items in his rucksack, went out onto his balcony and looked down. He was five floors up but this presented no particular difficulty, as he was an expert climber. He checked that no one was looking, then climbed over the railing and lowered himself down so that he was dangling a few feet above the balcony below his own. The light was on inside, so he would need to be careful. He swung himself forwards and let go - dropping just within the railing of the lower balcony. There were voices - perhaps he had been heard. Without waiting to see if anyone would come to the window, he jumped across to the neighbouring balcony - Mr E's.

The curtains were drawn in Mr E's room but the light was off. Snipper used his pocket knife to lever the window open. Then he

slid the window back until there was just the tiniest crack of an opening and no cold draught to catch Mr E's attention. And now he waited - for over an hour in the freezing cold until, eventually, the light came on. He pricked up his ears: he could hear footsteps, then a squeak and two heavy thuds. From these sounds he worked out that Mr E had walked over to his bed, sat down and thrown off his shoes. Now came a jangle, a clunk and a rustling sound which lasted a couple of minutes: this, thought Snipper, was probably Mr E emptying the contents of his pockets onto a table and undressing. Then, at last, there was the click of a door and the sound of a shower running in the distance.

Snipper had read somewhere that ninety-eight per cent of hedgehogs take between five and ten minutes in the shower. That gave him five clear minutes. For the first thirty seconds, he remained on the balcony just in case Mr E returned to the bedroom to collect something for his shower. The door, however, remained shut. So Snipper slipped in through the window. Though he had the sound of the shower to cover him, he nevertheless moved quietly as he made straight for the bedside table. The first thing he did there was to place the candle from his rucksack on the table and light it. Leaving the wax to soften, he then turned his attention to the glass of water on the table. There were several pawprints on the glass; Snipper applied the tape to the best of these and then returned the

tape to its backing and his rucksack. Next he checked the candle. There was enough melted wax for his purpose. So he took the candle to the window, pinched out the flame and wafted the smoke away with his paw. Next he poured the melted wax into his tin lid. Leaving this to one side, he then photographed Mr E's passport, credit cards and three crumpled receipts. Interestingly, the passport and two of the credit cards were in the same name as he had given the receptionist - Signor Pungolo - but the third card was in the name of Monsieur Gratton. Snipper glanced at the candle: the wax was just the right consistency now. Picking up Mr E's keys, he pressed them against the tin lid one by one, making a clear impression in the soft wax. He then returned the lid to his rucksack. The final item on Mr E's bedside table was his mobile phone. Snipper scrolled through the messages - which were in several different languages. With just three minutes left, he went as fast as he could - but then stopped dead.

*Hedgehog called snipper on my tail,* read one of the outgoing messages in Hedgelandish. *No photo or description. Travelling with at least 2 others - they do not seem to be involved.*

There was a reply: *Snipper not known. Suggest you take no risks.* But it was Mr E's response to this suggestion that he take no risks which sent a real shiver down Snipper's spines:

*Shall get rid of snipper & companions. Shall make it look natural.*

30

Snipper noted down the telephone number of Mr E's contact. Next he inserted the SIM card from Mr E's phone into his own and copied the contact list. When he had returned both card and phone, he checked his watch: he calculated he had another fifty seconds left. He went over to the dressing table, on which there lay a large brown envelope. Inside the envelope were several odd-looking maps all entitled *7.2m Rise*. He photographed the maps and returned them to their envelope. Now he had just forty-two seconds left. The drawers and wardrobe were empty but a set of clothes lay draped over a chair and the monogrammed cufflinks were still in the shirt. Snipper photographed the monogram and the hallmark on the back. Then he made a start on Mr E's suitcase. There were skiing clothes, climbing equipment and a gun. Snipper made a note of the gun's serial number but now he had just seven seconds left. He put the case back exactly as he had found it, picked up his own belongings and slipped out of the window.

Back in his own room, Snipper sat on his bed and frowned. Mr E would not be the first hedgehog to try to do away with him, but this time his enemies were out to get his friends, too. He wondered whether he should come clean with Pawline and Scratch - tell them he was a secret agent and that, because of his job, someone was trying to kill them all. He wondered, too, if they would ever trust him again once they knew he had been lying to them all these years. The lengths he had gone to in order to pull the wool over their eyes somehow made it seem worse - the fact that the lies were so detailed, with all his talk of Tippuyu pots and important clients in Hogotà. Now their very lives were at risk because of him. They would surely hate him. But that was beside the point: it was his responsibility to protect them and, if he had to lose their friendship in the process, it was a price he would have to pay.

Snipper brushed away these unhappy thoughts and emailed Secret Service H.Q. with an update on his situation. He also sent the telephone numbers and photographs he had taken. Then he lay back on his bed and thought about what he had learned so far.

First of all, Mr E was using at least two names - Signor Pungolo and Monsieur Gratton. Snipper suspected that both were false as neither began with the letter E. This was not surprising as many criminals use false identities, but it was surprising to use two different nationalities. Was he Itchalian or Furzish? Or perhaps

some other nationality altogether? At the very least it suggested he must be fluent in two languages.

Secondly, Mr E clearly still had no idea what Snipper looked like: *No photo or description,* the text had read. Despina knew but had not told him. Perhaps Snipper had been wrong about her. He thought back to the masked stranger who had left her such a generous donation in Vertice. There was no actual evidence that this had been Mr E; and the suspicious behaviour Snipper thought he had observed could have been a trick of the imagination. He thought he had seen the stranger pick an envelope out of the collection box; but his paws had been empty when he turned round. Afterwards, in the alleyway, Snipper thought he had glimpsed a gun in the stranger's paw but even at the time he had been unsure; it had been dark, after all, and then Pawline had come between them. The fact that Despina had spoken to Mr E briefly on the train, when he picked up her book, began to seem increasingly like nothing more than politeness between strangers.

Snipper then turned his attention to the photographs he had taken of the maps in Mr E's room. When he had first glanced at them, he had easily recognized Great Bristlin, Itchaly and other parts of the world. However, their coastlines were strangely mis-shapen. Now, on closer examination, he realized the countries shown in these maps were suffering from serious flooding: huge swathes of low-lying land were shown under water. Vertice had disappeared and much of Snipper's own city had gone. The words *7.2m Rise*, which appeared at the top of each map, were now chillingly clear: this was the world as it would appear following a rise in the sea level of 7.2 metres.

In another hedgehog's paws these maps would have seemed wholly innocent: many scientists, environmentalists and politicians would be interested in them for the best of reasons. But, in the paws of a criminal mastermind like Mr E, they were far more likely to have a sinister purpose. A terrible thought crept into Snipper's mind. Could Mr E, for some devious criminal purpose of his own, actually be plotting to raise the sea level? The idea seemed preposterous and he tried to think of some other reason why Mr E might be interested in the maps. But, however hard he thought, he kept on coming back to the same point. He did not know why, how or when but he did know that, if Mr E wanted the sea level to rise, he would not be waiting for the climate to warm up.

Snipper's phone beeped. It was a message from Pinmoney at H.Q.. She reported that there was no record of any hedgehog called Despina in Secret Service files. Mr E, however, was the spitting

image of a shady character from Hogotà called Rasguno. Rasguno was suspected of acting as middle hedgehog between gangs of drug traffickers. About a year ago, while visiting Bristlin, he had been tailed by the Secret Service. The surveillance photograph - which Pinmoney had sent Snipper - showed Rasguno taking a briefcase from an unpleasant character called Snuffles.

It looked as though Mr E was going to be difficult to pin down. He was not only operating under multiple identities. He clearly also had a talent for languages, and this enabled him to assume different nationalities. Snipper wondered which name, if any, was his real one. He rather suspected they were all aliases, as surely his real name must begin with the letter E.

The other news from H.Q. concerned the sender of the text suggesting that Mr E take no risks. The sender's phone number was registered to none other than Gotha-Hölhog of 23 Dornig Straße, Bad Igel, Hedgermany. Gotha-Hölhog was one of the criminal masterminds listed in the report Dirkby had got Snipper to read before he went on holiday. He had started his criminal career as a supplier of CCTV, alarms and other security systems to wealthy businesses - which he then went on to rob. He now acted principally as a security adviser to criminal outfits all over the world.

The following morning, the weather experts announced that it was now safe to travel. The railway re-opened, and hotel guests travelling to Clawtina were told to gather at the front of the building at eleven o' clock; a shuttle bus would collect them and take them to the station. As they waited, Snipper looked round for Despina and Mr E. She was there but there was no sign of him. Snipper nipped back into the hotel: Mr E's room key was hanging up behind the reception desk. It looked as though he had already left. Whatever the case, he clearly had no intention of getting back on board the Vertice-Clawtina train. Given his text to Gotha-Hölhog saying he would get rid of Snipper and his friends, this was surprising but good news. For the time being at least, it looked as though they were safe. Snipper decided to keep a look out in case Mr E got back on board at another station. If he did, Snipper would tell his friends all. Otherwise, he would keep quiet - and keep their friendship.

As they walked down the platform towards the train, Snipper kept an eye on Despina. Unlike yesterday, they were free to sit anywhere since their seat reservations were no longer valid. He decided that, if at all possible, he would sit next to Despina. He was lucky. Despina was one of the first hedgehogs to board the train and she sat down in a group of four empty seats. Snipper followed swiftly behind, beckoning his friends to follow.

"Hallo! Fancy bumping into you again!" said Snipper. "Do you mind if I join you?"

"Snipper!" said Despina, with a look of faint surprise. "Please, you are welcome."

Snipper pretended to hesitate: "Actually, perhaps I'd better sit elsewhere. There are three of us travelling together, and I expect you're probably keeping a seat for your friend."

"My friend-a?" repeated Despina. "But I am travellin' alone."

"Oh, I thought you were with the hedgehog in the grey suit," said Snipper, testing the water. "The hedgehog who sat opposite you yesterday?"

"No, as I say, I am alone," insisted Despina.

Snipper could detect no hesitation or hint of confusion. She certainly sounded as though she was telling the truth. Dropping the matter, he smiled and sat down opposite her. As he did so, Scratch and Pawline boarded the carriage, looking around for him.

"Over here!" he said, raising his paw to catch their attention.

They deposited their bags in the luggage rack and joined him.

"I must say, Snipper," said Scratch sharply, "this is quite an annoying habit you seem to have developed - charging on ahead without even telling anyone where you're going. It's going to be a nightmare if you carry on like this when we're skiing."

"You've got to be kidding me! He's not *this* fast on skis!" joked Pawline, who had not seen Snipper ski since their university days.

Snipper thought he detected a hint of curiosity on Despina's face. "Scratch, Pawline," he said, ignoring his friends' remarks, "may I introduce you to... er... actually, I don't think I quite caught your name?"

"Despina. 'Ow do you do?"

35

"Oh!" said Scratch, turning to Despina with surprise; if he had known Snipper had company, he would never have told him off like that. "Delighted to meet you," he said, offering her his paw.

"Hey," said Pawline with a wave of hers.

"So, where are you travelling to, Despina?" asked Scratch.

"Clawtina," responded Despina briefly.

"Say, so are we!" said Pawline, "We're staying with a friend there. She and Snipper did History together at university. Why don't you swing by some time? I'm sure she wouldn't mind. Snipper can give you his cellphone number."

"Oh!" said Despina, who seemed a little surprised by this suggestion. "Yes, I will put de number on my telephone." She got her mobile out and tried to switch it on but nothing happened.

"What's the matter? Is the battery dead?" asked Pawline.

"I tink so, but it is no problem - I will write de number de old-fashion way," said Despina, who now produced a scrap of paper from her bag.

"Actually, I'm not sure there's much point, anyway," said Snipper, trying to get out of this. "I don't think my phone will work in the mountains." It seemed to him that Despina had so far shown no interest in making friends; so her interest in his phone number had re-awoken his suspicions. If she wanted his number, it was surely only to pass it on to Mr E.

"Of course it will work!" said Scratch. "There's loads of coverage nowadays. Surely you must have used your mobile in the mountains before?"

Snipper shrugged his shoulders and gave Despina a number very similar to his own - crossing his claws and hoping his friends would not notice the deliberate error. They did.

"That's not right!" said the sharp-witted Pawline. "You've got the last two digits the wrong way round." She gave Snipper a look which suggested that this was further evidence of his scatter-brained tendencies.

"Have I? I'm sorry - stupid me!" said Snipper, forcing himself to smile. He now repeated his phone number the correct way round. Then he asked Despina for hers.

"I am sorry," said Despina. "It is a new phone - I do not remember de number and, of course, de battery is dead so I cannot find out."

Snipper sighed inwardly. It was a good excuse and he wished he had been able to use it himself. However, with Scratch and Pawline present, it would not have been possible. Never before had he felt less in control of a situation.

"So, are you visiting friends in Clawtina, as well?" asked Pawline.

"My parents."

"Gee, that must be a cool place to live!"

"Oh, dey do not live in Clawtina - dey 'ave only de chalet for de ski. We go since I am born."

The conversation now settled down into general chit-chat. It turned out that Despina worked for W.I.S.C.A. - the World Institute for Scientific and Cultural Advancement. She was a scientist and part of a team of hedgehogs researching the reasons for the gradual sinking of Vertice. Though the city had, in fact, been sinking for centuries, the situation had now become so serious that its very existence was at stake. Snipper thought back to that evening in Vertice, when he had first come across Despina, busking with her friends in the piazza: they had been collecting money to help save the city. It was obvious that she cared very deeply about it.

Snipper would have liked to have heard more about her research. However, though her Hedgelandish was good, she seemed to have difficulty talking about such a complex subject in a foreign language. She apparently understood much more than she could say.

So Scratch and Pawline were soon telling her all about themselves. This was, of course, very interesting. It was therefore some considerable time before Despina finally turned to Snipper and asked him what he did for a living.

"Me?" said Snipper, startled out of a slight trance. He realized he had been staring at Despina and not listening to Scratch and Pawline at all. He hoped she had not noticed. "I... I'm an art dealer," he said, repeating the well-worn lie. He shifted awkwardly in his seat. He did not remember feeling this uncomfortable before. He was so used to leading a double life that he almost believed his cover story himself. The problem now was that, if Despina was working with Mr E, she would know he was lying. Was she? Did she? Snipper no longer knew what to think. According to an ancient proverb, you may judge a hedgehog by the company he keeps. But did she keep Mr E's company? Or had they just been strangers sitting together on a train?

"Dealer?" repeated Despina, who seemed unsure of the word.

"Yes, I buy and sell works of art and ancient artefacts - that's basically anything that's very old," explained Snipper. "It's absolutely fascinating. I get to see items that'll never be displayed in a gallery or museum. And no two days are the same: one day I might be looking at a pot from the Ancient Pinca Empire; the next I'm looking at a pot from the Ancient Pawsian Empire..."

Despina blinked heavily. If she thought he was lying, she ought now to be trying to pick holes in his story. Instead, she seemed to be trying hard to show an interest and not succeeding. As with Pawline and Scratch, this clearly did not come naturally. Not that many hedgehogs are that interested in pots. This was, of course, half the point of his cover story. It was *meant* to prevent other hedgehogs from taking too much of an interest in what he did. But sometimes it made him feel very alone. No one knew the real Snipper - not even Thistley, Scratch or Pawline, who were his closest friends. The Snipper they had known at university no longer really existed. In their eyes, he was the same as ever - a little bookish perhaps, but also very sociable and straightforward. However, four years in the Secret Service had changed him. He had much less time for reading now, was no longer the party animal he had once been and, with all the lies and subterfuge, could hardly be described as straightforward. His friends did not see it, though; and perhaps that was just as well.

38

Despina's eyelids drooped, flickered for a moment as she tried hard to stay awake and then shut tight. So that was that. Snipper turned to join in his friends' conversation. However, Scratch was busily explaining the principles of climbing to Pawline and, so far as they were concerned, Snipper had never climbed before. He decided not to join in the conversation after all: he was in no mood for further lies. Instead, he stared gloomily out of the window. It was snowing heavily. The leaden sky and the flat, featureless countryside of Itchaly's northern plain only reinforced his mood. He checked his watch: in a few minutes they would arrive in Lametta, and he would pass the case on to his colleague, Pierce. Then perhaps he could at least relax a little.

When the train drew into the station, Snipper scanned the platform for a hedgehog matching Pierce's description. Fortunately, there was only one hedgehog in a green coat and black trousers; so it had to be him. He boarded the train a couple of carriages along from Snipper but, according to standard procedure, would now be making his way to the buffet car. Snipper excused himself and went to join his colleague.

When he reached the buffet car, he found Pierce propping up the bar with a caffè corretto in his paw. Snipper did not acknowledge him immediately but ordered himself a cappuccino. Then, when the waitress turned her back on them to make the coffee, he spoke.

"It looks pretty chilly out there," he observed casually.

"Yes, it's good to come in from the cold," responded Pierce, brushing the snow from his shoulders.

Snipper did not reply. Contact had been made, and all further conversation would take place in private. Pierce picked up his coffee and left. Snipper stayed, gazing out of the window while the waitress frothed the milk. In the distance, the mountains were visible at last - bringing the plains to a sudden end. He smiled. After a couple of days on the ski slopes, perhaps this unsettling journey would seem like a distant memory.

"*Ecco, signore,*" said the waitress, producing his coffee. Snipper paid and then proceeded to the lavatory, where Pierce was waiting for him. It was a tight squeeze and not the most pleasant place for a meeting but the only one where they would not be overheard. He locked the door behind him.

"Good to meet you at last, Snipper," said Pierce, offering him his paw. "Dirkby speaks very highly of you."

"You've got quite a reputation, yourself," responded Snipper, as he shook the proferred paw.

"So, I gather you've stumbled across Mr E," said Pierce, getting straight to the point, "and a possible accomplice called Despina."

"Yes - not quite what I expected when I set out on holiday," observed Snipper. "I assume Dirkby's kept you up-to-date with what I've found out so far? And you've seen the maps? Good. I've also got a couple of items for you here which I couldn't send - Mr E's pawprint and a mould from a bunch of keys on his bedside table. Unfortunately, Mr E himself has disappeared, and I've no idea where he is except that it's not here on this train. Odd, given what he told Gotha-Hölhog."

"That he would kill you?"

"Yes - and my friends."

"Hm," mused Pierce, pawing the items Snipper had just given him. "You say Despina's still on the train?"

"Yes?"

"Perhaps Mr E has passed the task on to her."

This possibility had not occurred to Snipper. He had suspected Despina of working with Mr E but the idea that she might be an assassin somehow seemed preposterous. Of course, the first rule of espionage was to suspect everyone and trust no one, as he well knew. Yet, for some reason he could not quite put his paw on, he

40

felt annoyed with Pierce for making his suggestion. He hid his annoyance. "Well, as it happens," he said, "I managed to start a conversation with her and we're now sitting together."

"Nice work," said Pierce with a sardonic smile. "As they say, keep your friends close and your enemies closer. All the same, it's probably best if I keep an eye on her, too. You can stay up close, and I'll be a flea on the wall. If she's up to no good, we ought to nail her pretty quickly between the two of us."

Snipper did not much like the idea of having Pierce on his tail. But he had asked for Pierce and he had got Pierce; in any case, he was a safe pair of paws and the plan was sound. So Snipper agreed to the plan and returned to his friends. Pierce followed on a couple of minutes later and found himself a seat nearby.

"You seem very restless, Snipper," said Pawline as he reappeared. "There isn't anything bothering you, is there?"

"No, I'm fine," said Snipper, glancing out of the window. They were in the mountains now. It had stopped snowing but the fresh powder was heavy on the trees. Far above, rocky peaks soared up into an intense blue sky; while, below, the glare of the white snow was almost dazzling. Snipper turned back to Pawline. "I just wanted to stretch my legs," he explained.

"I thought you might be worrying about the avalanche business."

"No, not really. They said it was safe, and I don't think they'd take any risks."

"I guess not," said Pawline.

"No, dey would not," said Despina, who was awake again. She spoke emphatically, like a hedgehog who knew what she was talking about.

"So, Despina, how long will you be staying in Clawtina?" asked Snipper.

"Jus' for one week."

"And your parents? You said they were already there - are they taking a longer holiday?"

"Yes, dey are already in Clawtina since one week and will stay for one more."

"That's nice for them," said Snipper. He paused for a moment, not wishing to sound as though he were interrogating her.

" 'Ow long will you stay wid your friend?" asked Despina.

41

"We've got the whole week," said Pawline. "I've flown over from the United Stakes especially. I haven't seen Thistley in over a year, so I'm real excited."

"From the United Stakes? So you are not Bristlish?

"No. I just did my degree in Bristlin - that's where I met these guys."

"You were all studying de same subject?"

"Not all of us," said Scratch. "Snipper and Thistley both did History. I did Engineering and Pawline did Astro-Physics."

"What's your specialism, Despina?" asked Snipper. "I mean, I know you're a scientist but presumably there's a number of different sciences involved in a project like yours?"

"Yes, dere are actually quite a lot - geology, sedimentology, geomorphology, climatology, engineering geology..." She paused and stared at the ceiling as though trying to remember some others; Snipper got the distinct feeling that she was hedging.

"Mm, interesting," said Scratch, who was of course an engineer, himself. "I fear it won't mean much to a non-scientist like Snipper, though. I think he really just wanted to know what *your* field is."

"Field?" repeated Despina, as though she could not understand why they were suddenly asking her about fields. "Oh! You mean - "

She stopped mid-sentence. Snipper caught her eye. They had both

heard the same sound - a faint but distinct bang. They did not see it but above them, far up the mountain, a fountain of white powder reached high into the sky.

"What's the matter?" asked Pawline.

"It sounded like a distant explosion," said Scratch, leaning over to look out of the window. "Yes - look, they must be clearing the snow. It's awfully close."

"Whoa!" exclaimed Pawline as she followed his gaze. "Pretty cool, huh?"

Snipper watched as the mountain top appeared to mushroom and then plunge downwards like a huge wave, leaving large stretches of bare rock behind it. With the complicated ups and downs of the Altispine Mountains, it was difficult to see exactly where the wave was headed - or, for that matter, the train. He pressed his face against the window, trying to make it out.

"Dere is a bridge which we mus' cross soon," said Despina, reading Snipper's thoughts. "I know de area well."

"Can you tell where the avalanche is heading?" he asked.

Despina did not respond at first but carried on looking out of the window. When she did eventually turn round to answer him, she looked tense and grave. "De bridge I tell you about," she said,

43

speaking a little breathlessly, "under it is a... 'ow do you say? A ditch?"

"A gully," said Snipper helpfully.

"Yes, under de bridge is a gully which run down from de mountain from where de avalange is comin'. De snow, when it will come off de mountain, it will go into de gully."

"Are you saying it'll destroy the bridge?" asked Snipper, who feared the worst but wished to be absolutely clear.

"Of course it'll destroy the bridge," said Scratch. As an officer in the Royal Engineers of the Bristlish army, he had destroyed a few bridges himself. "No bridge could withstand an avalanche of that size. We need to stop the train before it gets there." He looked round for the emergency cord.

"No!" said Despina, putting her paw on Scratch's arm. "It is no' safe to stop 'ere. De gully is not enough deep for containing so much snow. If we stay 'ere, we will not escape de avalange. We mus' carry on up de mountain - we mus' cross de bridge."

"You've got to be kidding me!" protested Pawline in disbelief. "You want us to go ploughing on towards that giant wall of snow? I mean, if it's not safe to stop here, then let's go back the way we came!"

"No, we shall only be safe when we shall be above de avalange. If we go back, we go down. But, if we go faster, we can be over de bridge-a before it will be destroyed," said Despina.

As she spoke, there was a screeching of brakes. The hedgehogs were thrown forward as the train suddenly came to a halt. Clearly, the driver did not know the area so well as Despina. Like Scratch and Pawline, his instincts had been to stop the train. Despina jumped to her feet.

"Where are you going?" exclaimed Snipper, fearfully. It was irrational, of course, but somehow he felt she would be safer if she stayed with them.

"I am going to speak to de driver," she said with gritty determination. Then she hurried out of the carriage. Snipper wondered if he would ever see her again.

"Right, it's high time we spoke to the other passengers," said Scratch. "Somebody ought to take charge or it'll be pandemonium in here."

"If there's nothing we can do, how's speaking to the rest of the passengers gonna help?" asked Pawline. "Anyway, I reckon most of them have already worked it out for themselves: you don't have to speak the lingo to hear the rising panic in their voices."

"We can still let them know the drill," said Scratch. "We should get them down on the floor and holding onto something. Snipper, you'll have to transl - "

"What's going on?" It was Pierce, who had just got up from his seat. Sitting across the gangway from them, he had listened to their conversation with growing concern but had been unable to see the avalanche for himself. Now, as he looked through their window and saw the snow crashing down the mountainside, he could see they had not been exaggerating the danger.

"I see," he said gravely, as he turned to face the group of friends. "Well, I can speak to the other passengers for you, if you like - I speak the language fluently." He exchanged the briefest of looks with Snipper, but there was no need for them acknowledge each other. Then he turned to face the rest of the carriage: *"Attenzione, signori, c'è una valangia..."*

There were gasps and, somewhere at the back of the carriage, a hedgehog started to cry. Generally, however, Pierce's words appeared to have a calming effect. In any case, one by one, the passengers did as they were advised, got down on the floor and held on to whatever they could. Heeding his own advice, Scratch also got

down on the floor. Pawline followed suit.

As she did so, the train began to move again - slowly at first but then building up speed until it was going much faster than before. Snipper and Pierce looked at each other but neither said a word: so Despina had got to the driver - but they were not over the bridge yet.

Now Pierce got down, but Snipper paused a moment and took one last look out of the window. The first few carriages were on the bridge now and suddenly the huge wave of snow was coming directly towards them - crashing down the gully, bringing boulders and uprooted trees in its wake. He squeezed down into the narrow space between the chairs and waited.

The noise of the approaching avalanche was immense now - a deep deafening rumble which sent shivers down Snipper's spines. He breathed in deeply as he waited. A young hoglet whimpered as its mother clutched it to her. He looked round and wished there were something he could do. Then his thoughts returned to Despina. If only...

Suddenly Snipper felt the train veer to the left. He got up from the floor to see what was happening. The last carriage had left the bridge, and the train was now running alongside the gully. Just a few feet below them, the snow was sweeping down the mountain with unbelievable power. Looking back, he saw the bridge crushed by the

force of the avalanche and the snow spilling up over the sides of the gully as it got shallower.

Then he looked ahead again. He noticed that, just to the left of the railway tracks, the ground rose to form a low ridge - creating a barrier between the train and the gully. He began at last to breath more easily and was about to tell the others the danger was past when he felt the driver slam on the brakes. Looking again, Snipper now saw that the track ahead was covered in snow: there was a cleft in the ridge he had not seen, and the avalanche had come through it. He immediately dropped back onto the floor and grabbed a chair leg with both paws.

A second later, the train slammed into the snow bank, throwing its passengers forward. A hedgehog let out a piercing shriek as a suitcase fell on him. Then the lights went out. Suddenly everything was still: the steady roar of the avalanche surging down the gully below was the only sound. Snipper looked round for his friends. They were unhurt - though the tension on their faces was plain enough. For a few seconds, neither they nor anyone in the carriage spoke or moved.

Finally, however, Pawline began to stir. "Is it over?" she asked. She raised herself onto her knees. Just as she did so, the noise of the avalanche grew suddenly louder.

"Get down!" said Snipper sharply.

Pawline did not wait to be told twice. As she dropped back onto the floor, the roar of the avalanche became thunderous. The next moment, a fresh wave of snow surged over the edge of the gully and through the cleft. It crashed down onto the train from above and knocked the carriage over onto its side, sending hedgehogs and luggage flying. Snipper could feel the carriage starting to slip down the snow bank. Hedgehogs cried out screaming and sobbing. And still the snow continued to thunder down on them - until at last it blotted out the sky and they were left in darkness. Then the sliding stopped and a minute later the roar of the avalanche died away. There was silence - real silence this time. For a terrible moment Snipper wondered whether he was the only hedgehog left alive. Then someone moaned in pain nearby. Further off a hoglet began to cry.

"Pawline? Scratch?" said Snipper softly. "Are you all right?"

"I'm good," said Pawline. "Scratch, are you there?"

"Um... all... all present and corr... correct," said Scratch in a distant voice which suggested that all was far from correct.

"You don't sound so great," said Pawline. "Hold on while I get my flashlight and first aid kit."

"You bring those things on holiday?" queried Snipper, surprised.

"Yeah, sure. I like to be prepared when I go skiing. Here we are," she said, turning on her torch. She pointed it at Scratch, who blinked painfully in its glare. The fur on his forehead was matted with blood. "Hm, that's a nasty cut on your forehead, Scratch. Does it hurt?" Scratch murmured something incomprehensible. "I think he's got concussion," she said, looking at Snipper with a worried expression. "It could be serious. Once I've dressed this wound, I'll need to put him in the recovery position."

"Can I help?" asked Snipper.

"No, I should be all right. I've had basic medical training - all astronauts get that. Why don't you check whether any of the other passengers need help?"

"OK. Let me know if you need me."

"Likewise."

Using the light from his mobile phone, Snipper picked his way carefully through the debris of the carriage. "Pierce!" he whispered. "Pierce, can you hear me?"

"Over here!" responded a weak voice.

Snipper moved towards the voice. "Are you hurt?"

"Cracked rib, I think, but I'll live. Are your friends all right?"

"Well, Pawline's fine but Scratch has concussion. I don't know about Despina - she left the carriage before the avalanche hit..."

49

Snipper's voice tailed off but then he added: "This was no accident, you know."

"I agree," said Pierce, shifting uncomfortably.

"At least that puts Despina in the clear," said Snipper. "She'd never have got back on the train if she'd been working with Mr E."

"It seems unlikely," agreed Pierce. "All the same, right now we've got other problems."

"Yes, I'm sorry. Can you move?"

Pierce nodded painfully, and the two hedgehogs crept through the darkness, looking for casualties. To their immense relief, no one had been killed. However, there were several broken bones among the passengers and several cases of concussion. It was a worrying situation. Pawline was doing a great job but she was no doctor, and there were hedgehogs in need of proper medical attention. In the other carriages, it might be worse. There was also a possibility that the avalanche might start off again: it was too soon to be sure the snow had stabilized.

Snipper got his telephone out to call the emergency services. However, there was no reception. The same went for Pierce and the other passengers. Either the masts were down or there was no coverage in this area.

"Do you have any idea where we are?" asked Snipper. Pierce had already been in Itchaly, on another mission, when he had been asked to help out; so Snipper hoped he might have picked up a little local knowledge.

"No, I'm afraid not," said Pierce. "My last mission didn't take me this far north. But let's see... the train isn't due in Clawtina until 15.50 hours and there aren't any more stops before that; so, unless someone heard the avalanche or the driver's managed to get a message out, we won't be missed for another three hours."

"Well, *I* didn't see any villages from my side of the train when the avalanche struck," said Snipper. "So, if you didn't either, I doubt there was anyone close enough to have heard it. But there's bound to be a village somewhere down in the valley - or at the very least a farm or two. I'll ski down and raise the alarm."

"I'll come with you," said Pierce. "It mayn't just be a matter of skiing. If there's any climbing involved, it'll be a lot safer if there's two of us."

"Out of the question," said Snipper. "With your broken rib, you'll be a lot more use if you stay here and translate for Pawline."

"All right - fair enough," said Pierce reluctantly, "but one of the other passengers should go with you. We can ask around and see if any of them are expert skiers and climbers."

"Too risky," said Snipper, shaking his head. "They might not be quite as good as they think they are, and then they'll just be a hindrance. I'm better off alone."

Pierce sighed but in the end he had to agree. They were, after all, both S.L.U.G. agents and used to working on their own.

So the two hedgehogs parted. When Pierce found Pawline, she accepted his offer of help gratefully. Snipper seemed to have gone astray yet again and this other hedgehog would probably be a lot more reliable. And so it seemed to prove, for they were soon working well together. Going round from hedgehog to hedgehog, Pierce found out who was hurt and how, while Pawline used her medical knowledge to dress the wounds. Before long she ran out of bandages and pins but she was a resourceful hedgehog: she used her scarf as a sling, tore up some shirts to make bandages and even pulled out a few of her own spines to use as pins.

Snipper, meanwhile, hunted round for his luggage. When he had found it, he took out his skiing things. Then he went into a private corner of the carriage to change. He put on his black ski trousers, yellow ski jacket and his snow boots, and stuffed his ski boots, sunglasses, goggles and gloves into his backpack. Next he looked for Scratch's bag. He seemed to remember that Scratch had been explaining the principles of climbing to Pawline earlier and thought there was a good chance he had brought his climbing equipment on holiday to keep his paw in. Knowing Scratch, who was easily bored, a whole week of just skiing would be too much - he would have to have something else to do to keep him going.

Snipper guessed correctly - Scratch *had* brought his climbing things with him. He transferred most of the equipment into his own backpack but looped the ice-axe around his wrist. Then he helped himself to a pair of skis which looked the right fit and strapped these to his rucksack. Finally, he found a window away from the other passengers, climbed up onto a seat arm beneath it, placed his overcoat against the glass and smashed the window with the axe.

The glass shattered and, as Snipper removed his coat, it cascaded down into the carriage, followed by a flurry of snow. Several hedgehogs cried out, startled by the noise in the darkness. Then Snipper heard Pierce's reassuring voice respond - presumably explaining what Snipper was doing. The explanation seemed to satisfy all but one hedgehog.

When she heard the smashing glass, Pawline hastily finished the sling she was making for a hedgehog with a fractured arm. Then she picked her way along the carriage to where Snipper was poised below the broken window.

"Snipper, are you out of your mind?" she said, shining her torch at him. "What on earth do you think you are doing?"

"I'm going to get help," said Snipper, blinking in the glare of her torch. "We can't just stay here, you know."

"OK, but why you?" protested Pawline, who was astonished by what seemed to be most unSnipperlike behaviour. "There's no point risking your life when there's got to be better skiers here. There's a lot of deep powder out there. It's probably unstable and it's certainly dangerous. I don't want to be rude, Snipper, but it needs a really good skier... And what if it's steep or rocky or you come up against a cliff? You've never climbed before in your life."

"Actually, I've been taking lessons," said Snipper, with a faint smile.

"Don't fend me off with wisecracks!"

"But I have!"

"Well, OK then but you can't have been learning very long." She looked at him earnestly. "Sure, you want to be a hero - I get that - but this is nuts. You might die out there. Even if you're just forced to turn back, we'll have lost precious time. Come on, let's speak to the other passengers! There's bound to be some good skiers and climbers among them."

"Honestly, I'm a pretty good climber and a pretty good skier," said Snipper firmly. He turned away now. He could see he would never convince her without explaining he was a highly-trained S.L.U.G. agent. He put on his ski gloves and threw his coat over the jagged edge of the broken window glass to protect himself.

"Snipper!" cried Pawline in exasperation. "Are you even listening to me?"

Above the broken window was a small igloo-like hollow, where the snow had collapsed into the carriage. Hoisting himself up into this small space, Snipper sat for a moment, hunched over and with his legs dangling through the window. "I'm sorry, Pawline," he said, "we're going to have to finish this conversation another time."

52

With this, he pulled a small shovel out of his backpack and started tunnelling his way to the surface. As Pawline watched him, her frustration changed to sorrow. This behaviour seemed so unlike him. She could not figure it out at all; but she finally understood she was not going to change his mind.

"Snipper!" she called to him - gently this time. "Stay safe!"

He looked down at her and smiled. "I will," he said.

She smiled back sadly and then returned to her patients while he got on with his tunnelling. In five minutes, he was through. He stuck his head out and surveyed the scene. It was completely still out there. The smooth white snow left by the avalanche glistened in the sun, and everything looked strangely peaceful. But for an uprooted tree here and there, you would never have guessed that a devastating avalanche had just swept through. The train had been completely covered by the snow, but it could have been so much worse. The bulk of the avalanche had swept down the gully; the rest had lost much of its force when it had been pushed up over the ridge. They had missed disaster by a whisker. Had Despina not persuaded the driver to get the train over the bridge, it might have been a very different story.

Snipper threw his skis and backpack out of the tunnel and was about to pull himself to the surface when he heard Pierce calling him. So he slid back down again to see what he wanted.

"Sorry to delay you, Snipper. But, before you go, can we just revisit this question of who or what caused the avalanche? I mean, are you quite certain it was Mr E?"

"Absolutely certain," said Snipper. "Mr E said he would make our deaths look natural. He'd never actually seen me so the only way to be sure of killing me was to destroy the whole train."

"What about your friends? Hadn't he seen either of them?"

"Only Scratch - fleetingly. And, if you think about it, he would still have had to have tailed Scratch to identify me. He couldn't do that, because I knew what *he* looked like and would have spotted him in an instant."

"I see. Well, I suppose an avalanche would seem like the obvious solution to a twisted mind," said Pierce, "but he was taking an awfully big risk. And, as it turned out, it didn't work, but he'll still have the police after him for attempted mass murder. You have to ask yourself what could be so important to him that he'd be willing to kill so many hedgehogs for it."

"You do," said Snipper thoughtfully, "and I keep on coming back to those maps I found - the maps showing a rise in the sea level. If he really is planning to raise the oceans himself, then he's prepared to drown millions of hedgehogs. A couple of hundred passengers on a train would mean nothing to him."

Little shivers ran down Snipper's spines as he thought of it. In all his years as a secret agent, he had never come across anything so evil as this.

"Well, I'd like you to be wrong," said Pierce, "but what you say makes too much sense. I'd better not keep you any longer. After all, we're going to have to get out of here before we can do anything to stop him."

Pierce gave Snipper his paw and wished him good luck. Then he returned to Pawline and the injured. Snipper climbed back up the tunnel and pulled himself out. He put on his ski boots and skis and was about to push off when a sound behind him made him stop. He looked round.

"Despina!" he exclaimed with unhidden pleasure.

"Snipper!" exclaimed Despina in her turn. She, too, seemed genuinely pleased to see him. He wondered how he could ever have thought she was on Mr E's side.

"How did you get out of the train?" he asked.

"De same way as you, I suppose - outta de window. I am goin' to get 'elp."

Snipper noted that she had her skis on and a large backpack strapped to her back.

"That's great, Despina," said Snipper, impressed by her courage, "but there's no need. I'm going myself - "

"No, I go," responded Despina simply. "I know de area like de back of my paw."

"You do?"

"*Certo!* Do you?"

"Well, no, but I was planning to head down to the valley. There's bound to be a village or a farm there. Of course, if you know somewhere closer, that would be really useful but you can just point me in the right direction. You don't need to come yourself. You've already done more than enough: getting the driver to speed up probably saved a great many lives. And it's dangerous out here - there's a real risk of setting off another avalanche. I'm used to skiing in difficult conditions…"

"I also," cut in Despina, "and I know to climb. Dere is a village over dere" - she pointed with a claw - "callèd Tagliento, where my cousin live, but we must go down onto a glacier, cross de glacier and den climb-a de cliff on de odder side. Do you know to climb?"

"Yes, I do but - "

"Dat is where I go now. It take abou' two 'ours. You can follow me, if you like-a."

Despina pushed off on her skis before Snipper could say another word in protest. However, his annoyance soon faded when he saw her ski. She really was good - as good as any S.L.U.G. agent. For a couple of seconds, he stood admiring her glide effortlessly down the mountain. Then he pulled himself together and pushed off in her tracks.

Snipper would have liked to know exactly where this village was. And he would have liked not to have the worry of his friends and the other passengers stuck on the train. Yet, despite all this, he was enjoying himself. The two hedgehogs skied in perfect harmony, slipping down the mountain at enormous speed together. Neither

had to stop and wait for the other, and Snipper kept so close that the fur on his face soon became damp with the spray from Despina's skis.

" 'Ere we are," said Despina, stopping abruptly. Snipper dug in his skis and drew up next to her. A few feet ahead of them, the piste suddenly disappeared. "Now we mus' take off our skis an' abseil down," she explained, pointing to the cliff edge. Snipper slid forward and looked down. It was nearly vertical, and in the u-shaped valley far below was a huge glacier full of gaping crevasses.

"So we cross the glacier and climb up the other side?"

"Yes. Den we ski down to Tagliento. I will show you on de map."

"You have a map!" exclaimed Snipper. "You seem extraordinarily well prepared."

"My cousin live in Tagliento, as I tell you. I alway bring a map when I visit de Altispina Mountain." Despina took out her piste map and a red biro. "So, we are 'ere," she said, marking the spot with a red X, "and we mus' cross de glacier 'ere - you see? It is written *ghiacciaio:* dat is Itchalian for glacier. Den we climb 'ere and we ski down to Tagliento where dere is an S.O.S. and an 'elicopter." She marked the route with red arrows and passed the map to Snipper. "You keep," she said, "I do not need."

Snipper put the map away in his pocket. They then swapped their skis, ski boots and poles for crampons, climbing boots and ice-axes

56

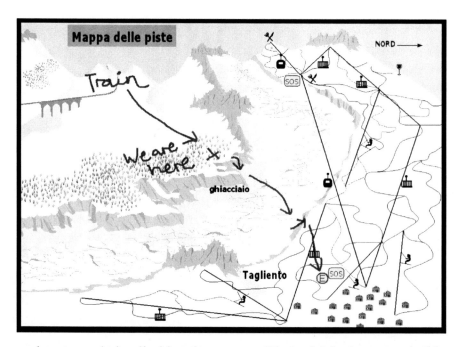

Mappa delle piste

NORD →

Train

We are here

ghiacciaio

SOS

Tagliento

SOS

and put on their climbing harnesses. Their ski boots went inside their rucksacks, while the skis and poles were strapped onto the outside. Despina led the way. Finding a slab of bare rock jutting up through the snow, she hammered a piton into it, attached a rope and then flung both ends of the rope over the cliff. Next she attached herself to the rope and, walking over to the very edge of the cliff, swivelled round so that she was facing Snipper. Then she stepped back and dropped out of sight.

Snipper walked to the cliff edge and watched her abseil down with impressive speed - feeding the rope through her paw with one smooth, continuous motion. There was no hesitation in her movements: she had the confidence of a seasoned climber and, within a couple of minutes, was down. Now she took herself off the rope, and it was Snipper's turn. He attached himself to the rope and stepped over the cliff edge.

Descending rapidly, he did not immediately hear the faint rumble above him. But then the sound grew louder and he pricked up his ears. He called out to Despina but there was nothing he could do to help her. So he swung himself in towards the cliff and clung to the rock face. The next moment, a small avalanche surged over the cliff edge; snow and boulders cascaded past him. A stone grazed his face and another hit his back but the overhang shielded him from the worst. Looking down, he saw Despina plunge her skis into the snow

and roll into a ball to protect herself; the next moment she had disappeared behind the wave of snow.

The whole thing lasted less than a minute. As soon as it had stopped, Snipper scanned the valley floor, looking for Despina. A little way off to his right, her skis were poking out of the snow; but there was no sign of Despina, herself. The avalanche had been much smaller than before and seemed scarcely big enough to bury a hedgehog completely. Yet, coming over the cliff edge like that, it had had tremendous force. Fighting off the terrible thought that she must have been swept down into one of the glacier's gaping crevasses, he abseiled down to the bottom of the cliff at lightning speed.

"Despina!" he shouted, as soon as he was down. He scanned the area again, desperately looking for her, but there was still no sign. "Despina!"

"Down 'ere!" Her voice was strained and muffled - coming from somewhere below him. Puzzled and fearful, he followed the direction of her voice and found himself walking towards a crevasse at the edge of the glacier.

Then he saw her. He was torn between relief and alarm: she was alive but wedged precariously inside a deep crevasse. The narrow neck of the crevasse had broken her fall and stopped her from plunging to the bottom – and her certain death.

"Go away!" ordered Despina, when she saw Snipper, "It is no' safe! Dere is - 'ow you say?..."

"An overhang?"

Despina nodded.

"Never mind," said Snipper, "I'll rope up."

He went back to the base of the cliff to retrieve the rope and then returned. A few feet from the crevasse opening, he plunged his skis deep into the snow, to form an anchor. Then he attached the rope to his skis, himself to one end of the rope and threw the other end into the crevasse.

"Despina!" he shouted, as he sat down, bracing himself to take her weight. "The rope - can you reach it?"

"In a moment... but I 'ave first to move to de odder side!"

"Wait," said Snipper, alarmed that she might fall. "I'll come down and get you!"

"No! I can do on my own!" responded Despina obstinately. Without waiting for him, she gripped an ice-axe in either paw and then propelled herself over to the far side of the crevasse. As she hit the wall of ice, she sunk both axes and her crampons into its surface. Pausing for a moment to make sure of her grip, she then reached for the rope and attached herself to it.

"I'm ready!" she shouted up to Snipper.

59

Snipper pulled the rope and, as he did so, it cut right through the snow bridge, causing it to collapse. He was suddenly just a couple of feet from the edge of the crevasse. Below him, he saw the rope slacken but Despina had a good grip and did not fall. He pulled again, digging his crampons into the snow, and Despina began to climb. As she approached the top, Snipper held out his paw. She

thrust one axe back into the ice, let the other hang loose from her wrist and then took Snipper's paw in her own. As she climbed out, there was a cracking sound below. The two hedgehogs peered down and saw a slab of ice come away from the neck of the crevasse; it tumbled out of sight and eventually, what seemed like minutes later, they heard it crash at the bottom.

Exhausted from their efforts, they now collapsed on the snow. For a few moments they lay there side by side, catching their breath and summoning up the energy to continue. Snipper wondered whether Despina would have the stamina to carry on. Yet he could not leave her here.

"Snipper," said Despina gently, interrupting his thoughts, "I am afrai' dat you are very tired - but really we should go now."

He looked round to find that she was already on her feet.

"No, I'm fine," said Snipper, leaping up. "Of course we must go."

Despina collected her skis. Then the two hedgehogs crossed the glacier carefully, roped to each other and always testing the solidity of the snow before they put their weight on it. It took them the better part of an hour to reach the other side. They then faced the tough climb up out of the valley. They made a belay and, without pausing for a rest, ascended the near-vertical cliff.

When they finally reached the top, the scene they met with seemed strangely unreal after all they had been through. A stone's throw away, a group of holiday makers was skiing a steep run with the kind of caution that follows a heavy lunch. A second group - hoglets fresh out of school - whizzed past them on their snow boards, whooping with excitement.

"Tagliento," said Despina, pointing.

Just beyond the skiers, was a busy little village bristling with holiday makers; to one side of the village was an S.O.S. station and a rescue helicopter - sitting there waiting for a call. Snipper and Despina skied down to the S.O.S. station and, fifteen minutes later, were waving the helicopter off. They had wanted to accompany the crew to lend a paw with the rescue but the pilot seemed to think they would only get in the way.

"Well, I expect you'll be wanting to get going," said Snipper once the helicopter had disappeared over the horizon.

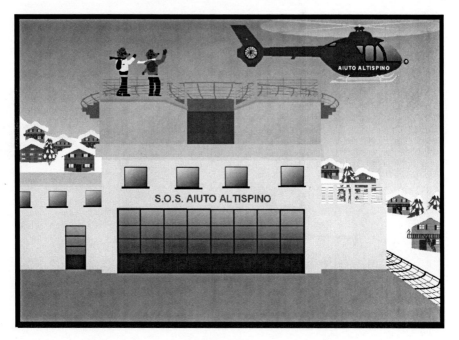

"No, I will wait," said Despina. "I would like to know dat your friends are OK."

"That's nice of you," said Snipper.

"It is de least I can do," said Despina, making it sound as though it were somehow her fault.

"I don't think you should feel any obligation to wait," he said. "You've just risked your life to get help. I'd say you'd earned enough brownie points for one day!"

Despina shrugged her shoulders. "Per'aps we wait-a from my cousin's place? 'E can give us someting to eat."

"Well, if you think he won't mind..."

" 'E won't," said Despina definitely. He had noticed that about her - she was always very sure of herself. She was right, of course: her cousin did not mind at all. The two hedgehogs had a pleasant lunch with him, and warmed themselves in front of a cosy log fire. When they had finished, though, Snipper began to feel restless, worrying about his friends. Despina seemed to read his thoughts and suggested they return to the S.O.S. station - to which he agreed readily enough.

Back at the S.O.S. station, they climbed up to the helipad and waited. It was late afternoon now and they watched as the last few skiers made their way home.

"So where do you go for your summer holidays?" asked Snipper, making conversation.

"Anywhere... nearly always a differen' place."

"Have you ever been to Bristlin?"

"Yes, I went wi' de orchestra of my university. We toured de country, visiting mostly de big cities."

"That sounds impressive," said Snipper, "though it's a shame if you didn't get to see the countryside. It's what I love most about Bristlin. There's nothing as high as your mountains but it's beautiful all the same - and great for walking. Do you like walking?"

"I don't know... yes, I suppose," said Despina, who sounded as though she thought this a novel idea.

Snipper wondered whether she would enjoy the day-long hikes he sometimes went in for. Then his thoughts wandered back to her trip to Bristlin with her university.

"Mandolins aren't normally played with an orchestra, are they?" he asked.

"Oh, you know I play de mandolin?" responded Despina, with a note of surprise. She had not mentioned the mandolin so far and had, in fact, played violin for her university orchestra.

Snipper hesitated for a split second. She did not know he had been there that night in Vertice - when her music had drawn him and Pawline out of the restaurant. "I saw your case on the train - it was mandolin-shaped," he said, by way of explanation, and then added: "I hope it hasn't been damaged."

"I also but, you know, we are lucky to be alive..."

Her voice tailed off and they were both silent for a while. They thought of Scratch and Pawline and all the other hedgehogs trapped on the train. Snipper looked out over the now empty ski slopes and wondered how the rescue was progressing. Despina shivered. There was an icy chill in the air.

"Would you prefer to wait inside?" asked Snipper.

"No, why?"

"I thought you were cold."

"No, I'm fine. I was just tinking about de avalange."

As she spoke, the rescue helicopter appeared over the horizon. There were a few tense minutes while they waited to see whether their friends were on board. Scratch was there - along with some other hedgehogs requiring urgent medical attention. However, they were relieved to hear that no hedgehog had been killed or critically injured. Then Pierce followed on the helicopter's next trip, and Pawline brought up the rear.

As soon as Scratch had been seen by a doctor and given the all-clear, the five hedgehogs were on their way again. Pierce said his goodbyes to Pawline and then, with a nod to Snipper, caught a bus back to Vertice. There was no point him continuing to Clawtina now that Mr E had disappeared and Despina was in the clear.

The others took the bus to Clawtina. It was dark now - and the end of a long and terrifying day; but Thistley was there to meet them, and there was something comfortingly normal about seeing her there, waiting for them in her red ski instructor's jacket. Despina's mother and father were there, too, and made a big fuss over her - much to her embarrassment. No one wanted to linger, though; so, once everyone had been introduced to everyone else, the party split and Despina left with her parents. Thistley naturally had a great many questions for her friends but, seeing how tired they were, she kept these for later and bundled them into her little car. Back at the chalet, she had a hot stew waiting in the oven, which they wolfed down with unusual relish. They then sat for a while, exchanging stories as they snuggled round a roaring log fire; soon, however, they could stay awake no longer and so retired early to their beds.

The following day, they were reunited with their luggage and able to resume their holiday. Snipper took no further part in the investigation into Mr E and Gotha-Hölhog. Other members of the Secret Service would take care of that now. At last, he was free to concentrate on his holiday and his friends - among whom he now counted Despina. Indeed, after all they had been through together, it seemed only natural for her to join them on the ski slopes. So, every morning, the five of them - Snipper, Despina, Thistley, Pawline and Scratch - would take the cable car up to the top of the mountain and do a couple of runs together. After that they usually split up. Scratch was taking it gently (the doctor had told him not to ski at all) and Pawline, who was not so good a skier as the others, was happy to keep him company. So, for the rest of the morning it was just Snipper, Despina and Thistley. Then, in the afternoon, Thistley would go off to teach her ski class, leaving Snipper and Despina to ski by themselves.

In the course of the week, Snipper found out a little bit more about Despina. He found out that she had played the violin in her university orchestra and taken up the mandolin later. Her favourite instrument, however, was the piano. She had none of her own but, whenever she visited her parents, she would spend hours playing on theirs or composing her own music. Despina, in turn, learnt that

Snipper was something of an artist. He could turn his paw to landscapes or portraits, and was equally at home in watercolours, oils, pastels or pencils.

The one subject they both seemed to avoid was work. However, work itself could not be avoided for ever and, all too soon, the week and the holiday came to an end. It was time to part.

"May I call you?" asked Snipper, as they waited at the taxi rank back in Vertice.

"Yes, I would like - in a mont' or so," said Despina.

"In a month or so!" repeated Snipper, slightly taken aback.

"Or I will call you - dat would be better. I mus' travel for my work an' my mobile phone don't work in all places."

Snipper thought that "a month or so" seemed a long time to be travelling for work; and surely her phone would not be out of range all that time. Although he had now managed to get her phone number, he could not help wondering whether she was trying to put him off.

"Oh, I see," he said - even though he did not. "It's funny - somehow I pictured you working in a lab - but maybe you do that, too. Whereabouts will you be going? Anywhere nice?"

"My office 'as not told me yet."

"Really? That seems a bit disorganized, if you don't mind me saying... Then again, I suppose it all depends on what exactly it is you do. Of course, you were about to explain that, weren't you, when the avalanche happened?"

"Yes, I was," said Despina slowly. She glanced towards Pawline and Scratch.

"OK, folks! This is us!" It was Pawline. They had reached the front of the taxi queue and Scratch was telling the driver to take them to the airport.

"Oh, already!" exclaimed Despina. "Den I mus' say goodbye."

Scratch offered her his paw: "Goodbye, Despina. It was really good to have you with us."

"Yeah, it was cool," agreed Pawline. "You'll keep in touch, won't you?"

"Of course!" said Despina. She proceeded to embrace them all in the Itchalian manner, pausing briefly when she came to Snipper. "I 'ope when we nex' meet it will be less... er... less difficult."

"Well, if you come to visit me, I think I can promise you there won't be any avalanches!" said Snipper jokingly.

Despina looked at him strangely - almost sadly. Then, with a final wave of her paw, she turned tail and left.

Part Two
Chapter One


As he travelled home, Snipper could not stop thinking about his unanswered question. He had asked Despina about her work twice now but each time they had been interrupted. He knew that she worked for W.I.S.C.A. (the World Institute for Scientific and Cultural Advancement) and he knew she was a scientist; but what sort of scientist exactly? He supposed it did not really matter; yet somehow it niggled.

Eventually, once he was home and concentrating on his own job, the question did fade from his mind. On his return to work, his boss, Dirkby, got him to reopen an old case. This was an unsolved leak of confidential documents from the Ministry of Information, which had occurred several years previously. Snipper worked on this for three months and made some progress. But the trail was pretty cold by now and he rather wished he were back on the tail of Mr E.

Then, just as Snipper was finally getting somewhere, Dirkby told him to drop the case. He now wanted Snipper to investigate Van Hogloot, the unofficial banker to a large portion of the criminal classes. The Top Secret report which Dirkby had told Snipper to read before his holiday had been all about Van Hogloot. According to that report, the previous six months had seen a significant spike in his financial activities. Among his ten principal clients over this period had been Gotha-Hölhog - the hedgehog whom Mr E had texted saying he would kill Snipper and his friends. Of the other names listed, some were known to Snipper but others were not. Instinct told him Mr E was on that list, whether under his real name or an alias; and, if so, an investigation of Van Hogloot might lead to Mr E - who had seemingly vanished into thin air after the avalanche.

Dirkby, however, was interested in Van Hogloot for his own sake. He had been looking for an opportunity to put a S.L.U.G. agent alongside him for some time. Now at last that opportunity had arrived: Van Hogloot was due to meet a new Bristlish client, a criminal called Pincher, whom he had never set eyes on before. Dirkby had decided that Snipper, who was not currently engaged on anything urgent, should take Pincher's place. Pincher would be arrested before he could board his train. Posing as Pincher, Snipper would then establish a working relationship with Van Hogloot; with time, he would be able to gain his trust and build up a full picture of his nefarious activities.

Dirkby had acquired his information by intercepting a small package which Van Hogloot had sent to Pincher. The package contained an invitation to meet him at his home in the Needlelands, along with some instructions on how to get there and a small key. According to the instructions, Pincher was to travel to a town called Doorndorp, where he would find a bicycle waiting for him; the key would unlock the bicycle. Inside the bicycle's basket, there would be an envelope and, inside the envelope, a map showing the way to the converted windmill where Van Hogloot lived. Following Van Hogloot's instructions to the letter, Snipper travelled to Doorndorp and took possession of the bicycle and the map.

As he rode out into the countryside, Snipper found that the wind was against him. Making progress was hard work, but the beauty of this blustery day more than made up for that. Small white clouds raced across the big open sky and, just ahead, a mass of tulips swayed in the wind. Keeping to the same canal towpath, Snipper passed through two villages and continued until he came to three black windmills, as described in Van Hogloot's letter. Here Snipper turned left onto a small wooden bridge. Then, having crossed the canal, he carried on down a narrow country lane until eventually he

came to a converted windmill surrounded by a white picket fence.

So this was Van Hogloot's home! It was charming and not particularly big - not an obvious choice for a criminal with international connections. But the instructions were clear enough, and Snipper was sure he had the right address. So he rang the bell and waited. The door was opened by Van Hogloot himself.

"Hallo, I'm Pincher," said Snipper, proferring his paw.

"Good. Please, komm in!"

They shook paws, and Snipper went inside.

"You vould like shomm tea?"

"Yes, please... and, I wonder, would it be possible to have a slice of bread and jam to go with it? Only that bicycle ride has made me ravenous!"

Van Hogloot nodded and disappeared into the kitchen to put the kettle on. Meanwhile Snipper took advantage of his absence to look around the room. It was a homely space with several comfy chairs and a fire blazing in the hearth. Above the fireplace hung an oil painting; it was a copy of a famous portrait known as *The Hedgehog with the Pearl Earring,* by the great Needlelander painter, Furmeer. Snipper, knowing quite a lot about art, inspected the painting closely. It was a very good copy. If the original were not hanging up in a public art gallery, Van Hogloot could undoubtedly have passed this off as the real thing; and, indeed, he could have sold it for a great deal more than it was worth.

"You Bristlish take milk and sugar in your tea - I am correct?" called Van Hogloot from the kitchen.

"Just milk for me, thanks."

Snipper heard the kettle coming to the boil and decided he had just enough time to peek into the adjoining room. He opened the door gently, so it would not be heard above the noise of the boiling water. It was a dining room, charmingly furnished in a manner reminiscent of a Furmeer painting. On its sturdy oak table stood an old-fashioned flagon and glass; and resting against one of the chairs was a lute. But the item which really caught his attention was the picture on the far wall.

It was a well-known painting called *The Concert*, also by Furmeer. In this case, however, the original had not been seen in public for years, for the simple reason that it had been stolen. Snipper felt sure that this was the original, and he was delighted. Here was some real hard evidence he could use against Van Hogloot. Until now, the Secret Service had possessed nothing which could be used against him in a court of law - shady though his banking activities undoubtedly were. Abandoning caution, Snipper went over to the painting and examined it with his expert eye.

71

"Vhat are you doing?"

It was Van Hogloot. He was standing in the doorway, with a gun in his paw.

"I was just admiring the painting," said Snipper airily, as though he had not noticed the gun. "It's very good, isn't it? In fact, so good I'd be willing to bet it's the original - though, as a rule, I'm not a betting hedgehog. That's worth quite a tidy sum - over a hundred million pounds, in fact. I hope you've got it insured?"

"Who are you?" snarled Van Hogloot.

"I work for the Bristlish Police - Art Squad."

Van Hogloot lifted the safety catch off his gun.

"I'd put that away if I were you," said Snipper. "You don't want to be charged for murder as well as theft, do you now?"

"Nobody vill hear de shots," retorted Van Hogloot. "Dere are no neighbours here."

"The police will hear - you don't imagine I just stumbled in here on my own, do you? I've been on your tail for some time. My visit is part of a joint operation between the Bristlish and Needlelander Police, and your home is surrounded."

Van Hogloot glanced out of the window. There was no sign of the police, but he would expect them to be well hidden. That meant he only had this hedgehog's word for it, and in the criminal world a hedgehog's word was worth little.

"Prove it!" he said. "For all dat I am knowing, you may be a tief yourself."

"I have ID," said Snipper reaching for the inside pocket of his jacket.

"Not so fast, Mr... whoever you are!" said Van Hogloot fiercely. "If dat is a gun for vhich you are reaching, you vill be dead before you vill be able to use it."

Snipper smiled in acknowledgement of this point. Then, very slowly, he put his paw inside his jacket and pulled out a warrant card. Van Hogloot took it and read:

*POLICE OFFICER*
*Warrant No. 7991 Detective Inspector Hobjay-Dart.*
*This is the warrant and authority for executing the duties of their office.*

Attached to the warrant card was a photograph of Snipper in police uniform. Detective Inspector Hobjay-Dart was one of the many aliases he used in the course of his work as a secret agent. The knowledge of art which he used to support his every-day cover, with friends and family, also meant he had little difficulty in passing himself off as a detective from the Art Squad. Had he reached for another pocket, other documents supporting other identities were also available to him. Right now, however, Detective Inspector Hobjay-Dart suited him perfectly.

"I am not going to let you to arrest me," said Van Hogloot, with an air of desperation now.

"No, I don't suppose you are," said Snipper, "and, fortunately for you, I don't want to arrest you. You see, I've got bigger fish to fry. What I want from you is information."

Snipper saw Van Hogloot's paw relax its grip on the trigger.

"Vhat sort of information?" asked Van Hogloot suspiciously.

"Why don't we discuss that over tea?" suggested Snipper with a smile, hoping now to put the discussion on a slightly more friendly footing. "Before it gets cold."

Van Hogloot frowned, puzzled that this police officer should be thinking of tea at a time like this. But the Bristlish were well known for their obsession with tea drinking, so perhaps this was just normal behaviour. Returning to the sitting room, Van Hogloot put away his gun and poured the tea. Snipper followed and helped himself to a cup. Then, after adding a little milk and stirring it for a few seconds, he produced a photograph of Mr E.

"I need to find this hedgehog," he said, passing the photograph to Van Hogloot, before taking a seat. "I believe he's a client of yours."

"Maybe he is; maybe he is not," said Van Hogloot, shiftily.

"You do know that you're going to have to do a lot better than that, don't you?" said Snipper. He tried to speak in as friendly a manner as possible.

"I am sorry, I cannot help you," insisted Van Hogloot. He grabbed his tea cup, which had started to clatter in its saucer; Snipper noticed his paws were shaking. "If my clients vill find out I am informing about dem, I am - how do you say? - a dead hedgehog... I vould be better off in prison."

"Not if we arrest your client first," said Snipper.

"But vill you? Dat may be your plan but you may fail. De risk is too big."

Snipper did not respond immediately. He gave his tea a vigorous stir. Then he got up and walked over to the window to think. Van Hogloot was clearly very frightened, and it was going to take more than the threat of prison to get him to talk. Gazing out of the window at the dead-flat landscape, Snipper reflected that the Needlelands was one of the lowest countries in the world - with much of it lying below the current sea level. If Mr E and Gotha-Hölhog succeeded in raising the sea by seven metres, two thirds of the country would end up under water - including Van Hogloot's windmill. It was therefore ironic that Van Hogloot should be the banker for this unholy project. It also seemed very unlikely that he would ever have got involved with Mr E and Gotha-Hölhog had he known what they were up to.

Snipper turned round and looked Van Hogloot directly in the eye. "I won't pretend it's without risk," he admitted, "though your identity as the source of this information will, naturally, be a closely guarded secret. However, if you don't help me, it's a dead certainty you'll go to prison; and when - eventually - you come out, you'll find your home has been swept away along with much of the rest of your country... that is, assuming you survive that long."

"Vhat do you mean?" responded Van Hogloot sharply.

"This hedgehog," said Snipper, tapping the photograph of Mr E with a claw, "and his chums are plotting to raise the sea level by seven metres. As I'm sure you don't need me to tell you, the Needlelands would experience the worst floods in its history should the plot succeed. Your property and the surrounding countryside would all be underwater... As," he added pointedly, "would many of the prisons be, too."

Van Hogloot stared at Snipper, aghast at the very thought of his home consigned to the waves forever. But should he believe him? The claim was surely preposterous. And why would the Art Squad be investigating such a plot anyway?

"You said you vere from de Art Sqvad," said Van Hogloot, and there was a note of challenge in his voice. "Vhat has any of dis to do vid *you*?"

"Nothing," said Snipper. "Nothing at all. Or so I thought. Until this week, in fact, I knew nothing of the plot. I was hot on the trail of the picture you stole; but yesterday I was called in by my boss. He filled me in on the bigger picture. He wasn't able to explain the reason for the plot - I don't think he knew - but no doubt there's some sort of profit to be made out of it. What he did tell me was that my help was needed to track down the ring-leaders' banker. He also told me in no uncertain terms that I would have to give up any idea of arresting you - *if* you agreed to spill the beans. I won't say I was happy about it - not after all those months of painstaking investigation... but we all have to consider the greater good every now and then, don't we?"

It was now Van Hogloot's turn to look Snipper directly in the eye. He considered the explanation for a minute. It appeared to make sense. At the very least, something had to be afoot that was considerably more serious than the theft of a one hundred million pound painting. Otherwise, Hobjay-Dart would surely have arrested him straight away. After all, he had had the advantage of surprise, and the place was surrounded.

Van Hogloot considered his options. Not co-operating meant arrest at best; at worst - if the police officer was telling the truth - his home and much of his beloved country would be destroyed. Co-operating, on the other hand, meant freedom from prosecution for theft; and, judging by the police officer's silence on the matter, there was no hard evidence which could put him away for his financial activities. But what if it got out that he was talking to the police? It was no good asking for police protection. He might just as well put up a sign declaring that he was a police informer! But he could always go away somewhere... just until this all blew over.

"All right... yes, I know dis hedgehog," said Van Hogloot, pawing the photograph. "But, if I tell you vhat you vant to know, I shall be forced to go away for a time. I vill need money."

Snipper knew very well that the one thing Van Hogloot did not lack was money, but this was no time to argue. "One thousand pounds," he said firmly, as though he would not make another offer.

"Dat vill hardly get me very far!" protested Van Hogloot. "Dis hedgehog whom you are seeking vill be a very dangerous enemy. If I betray him, I vill feel safe only vhen I am on de far side of de vorld... My ticket alone vill cost me several tousand pounds... and den I must pay for an hotel and a car. I could not survive for long on less dan tventy tousand."

"Done," said Snipper, who felt it was money well spent with the future of the world at stake. "The money will be in your account tonight. Now, how about that name?"

"His name is Heer Bernaald," said Van Hogloot at last. "I have his business card - here, take it. So, is dat all you vant? You vill go now?"

"That's all for now," said Snipper, taking the card.

"So, I can keep de painting?"

Snipper looked at Van Hogloot in faint surprise. He had very nearly forgotten all about the painting; but there was no way that Detective Inspector Hobjay-Dart would have walked out empty pawed. So he took the painting off the wall and made Van Hogloot wrap it up for him. Then he popped it on his bicycle and left.

Cycling away from the windmill, Snipper pedalled fast. It would not take Van Hogloot long to realize there was no police back-up - no officers hiding in the shrubbery outside his windmill. When, however, Snipper had at last put enough distance between himself and the windmill, he got off his bike and, sitting down on a grassy bank, read the card.

*Heer Bernaald, Scherpstraat 12, 1000NE Hogeveen, Naalderland.*

So here was yet another identity for Mr E - but none so far began with the letter E. Snipper wondered how on earth he would ever find out his real identity. Still, at last he had an address for his adversary.

Taking out his smartphone, he had a look at a map of the Needlelands. The town of Hogeveen lay to the north - not far away, but it was worth checking the address with H.Q. before going there. So he sent the details to Pinmoney and waited for her reply. It would do no harm to sit there for a bit, watching the boat sails gracefully gliding along the nearby canals. On a bright sunny day like today, a flat landscape like this came into its own. It was awful to think of it being swallowed up by the sea. He frowned at this thought and opened up Mr E's maps: as he had suspected, a seven metre rise in the sea level would leave Doorndorp well and truly under water; Hogeveen, however, would become a coastal town.

Snipper's phone beeped: it was Pinmoney with the information he had asked for. The Hogeveen address was a hotel; Heer Bernaald was its owner. He never visited but had his post forwarded to an address in Scrapejavik; this was the capital city of Icepeak, the island which Scratch had recently visited. Pinmoney had already run some checks on the Scrapejavik address. It was a small office, said her email, run by a single hedgehog who was apparently kept very busy. The local police reported that the office received a lot of visitors and a steady stream of deliveries. In view of this latest information, Snipper decided that Mr E was just using the Hogeveen address to cover his tracks. The office in Icepeak sounded much more interesting. He emailed Pinmoney back, asking her to book him a flight to Scrapejavik.

Pinmoney, however, declined - telling him instead to meet Dirkby by RV31 at 1900 hours that evening. RV31 was a park bench in Pawlement Hill Fields, a public space just a few miles from Snipper's home. So Snipper would have to postpone his trip to Icepeak. A little annoyed by this delay, he nevertheless returned to Bristlin and made his way to the meeting place - arriving a good half an hour before the arranged time.

The bench was already occupied, by a family of hedgehogs enjoying an evening out. Snipper waited nearby until eventually they left. Then he sat down in the middle of the bench and spread out his briefcase and newspaper beside him to discourage anyone else from sitting down. At 1900 hours precisely, Dirkby appeared at the bottom of the hill. Snipper picked up his newspaper and pretended to do the crossword while, out of the corner of his eye, he watched Dirkby approach.

"Good evening," said Dirkby as he sat down on Snipper's bench. He spoke quietly and without looking at Snipper. "Am I clean?"

"Yes, sir," said Snipper, still looking intently at his crossword.

"Are you sure?"

"Yes, sir," said Snipper, with an inaudible sigh. "I've got a good line of sight, and there's definitely no one on your tail."

"Good. So, Pinmoney tells me you've got hold of an address for Mr E. I must say I'm surprised Van Hogloot was prepared to give it to someone like Pincher."

"He knows I'm not Pincher."

"What!" growled Dirkby - he managed to sound angry even while talking in an undertone. "You mean to say you blew your cover at your very first meeting with him? This was a first rate opportunity, Snipper, and you've thrown it away!" He sighed. "I suppose I'll have to put someone else on the case now - someone a little more reliable."

"Sir, with all due respect, as a S.L.U.G. agent I'm expected to make my own decisions in the field. That list of Van Hogloot's clients included several of the biggest names in the criminal underworld, including Gotha-Hölhog. I felt certain Mr E had to be a client, too. Just a hunch, I know, but surely finding Mr E has got to come before everything else? I didn't think it right to pass up the opportunity."

"So, exactly how did you get him to co-operate?" asked Dirkby between gritted teeth.

"Well, first I threatened to arrest him for possession of a stolen painting and then -"

"Stolen painting? What stolen painting?"

"*The Concert* by Furmeer. It was stolen from an art gallery several years ago. You see, I had a bit of a snoop around Van Hogloot's place while he was making the tea, and there it was hanging up on his dining room wall right in front of me! I recognized it at once. So I threatened to arrest him if he didn't co-operate."

"And that did the trick?"

"Not quite - he was more frightened of Mr E than the prospect of prison. So I decided to tell him about Mr E's plot to raise the sea level. Given that two thirds of his country will end up under water - including his home - if Mr E has his way, that seemed like a pretty good motivator to me."

"I see," said Dirkby, tapping the bench impatiently with his claw. "So, he knows who you are and he knows we're investigating Mr E. Is there anything else you told him?"

"Not exactly," said Snipper, needled by the criticism. "In fact, I didn't really tell him who I was - I used my alias as Detective Inspector Hobjay-Dart. I did, however, tell him we would pay him twenty thousand pounds for travel expenses - so he can escape Mr E's wrath if need be."

"Twenty thousand pounds!" snorted Dirkby, who could not list generosity among his faults. "Where's he going - on a round-the-world cruise?"

"Quite probably, sir," admitted Snipper, with a hint of a smile.

"All right, Snipper, you've made a good case," conceded Dirkby at last, "and I assume we've got the painting back? That must be worth a bit."

"A hundred million pounds," said Snipper, trying not to sound too smug. "If you send a courier round, I'll see it's back in its owner's paws straightaway."

"Good, you do that. It wouldn't do for it to be stolen again while in your possession. In the meantime, I'll suspend the investigation into Van Hogloot and let you concentrate on Mr E. That is what you want, isn't it?"

"Yes, sir, thank you. I'd like to fly to Icepeak tomorrow morning, if that's all right. And I'll need Pinmoney to send me the duplicates of the keys I found in Mr E's hotel room. Is there any news from Pierce?"

"Yes, he's just sent in his report, as a matter of fact. He says Gotha-Hölhog recently bought up a swathe of land in the north of Hedgermany. More worryingly, he's also bought several thermite factories."

"Thermite?" repeated Snipper. "That's mostly used for welding or cutting metal, isn't it? For things like railway tracks?"

"Mostly, yes. But, tell me, what else do you know about thermite?"

"Well, it's a metallic powder. When it's lit, it produces a really intense heat - concentrated in a very small area. That's what makes it so good for cutting and welding. The army use it, too - for incendiary devices and destroying enemy equipment; but its military uses are pretty limited because it doesn't explode."

"Very good, Snipper. But you're wrong about one thing - or at least only half right. The army don't use it as an explosive; but, if you pour water onto burning thermite, it causes a steam explosion."

"It doesn't go out?"

"No, it doesn't; because the really special thing about thermite is that it contains its own supply of oxygen. That means it can't be smothered and can burn in almost any environment - even underwater."

"I see..." said Snipper, reflectively. "Sir, do we know how much ice would have to melt to raise the sea level by 7.2 metres?"

"We do. We've been doing some research. According to a very recent study by W.I.S.C.A. - yet to be published, in fact - a 7.2 metre rise is exactly what you'd get if all the ice on Gruntland were to melt."

"A study by W.I.S.C.A.?" repeated Snipper.

"Yes - the World Institute for Scientific and Cultural Advancement. You must have heard of it. Anyway, their office in Vertice has been looking into the effect of global warming on world heritage sites - places like Vertice, itself, in fact."

"Their office in Vertice?" repeated Snipper.

"Yes," confirmed Dirkby. "Look, is something the matter, Snipper? You're beginning to sound like my echo."

"Oh, I'm sorry, sir," said Snipper, snapping out of it. "Only I have a friend in Vertice - a scientist - and she works for W.I.S.C.A.."

"You think she's the hydrologist who did the study?" asked Dirkby.

"I'm not sure," said Snipper frowning. "She never really said what field she was working in. I did ask her but somehow I never got an answer."

"Well, never mind, if it is her, she's obviously working for a very good cause. I can't see what there is to frown about. I mean, there's certainly nothing very sinister about it, is there now?"

"No, nothing sinister whatever," agreed Snipper doubtfully.

Snipper arrived in Icepeak the following morning and was met at the airport by a plain clothes police officer called Ójafn.

*"Goðan daginn!"* said Snipper, giving the typical Icespeak greeting. *"Eg er Snipper."*

*"Goðan daginn, Snipper. Eg er Ójafn,"* said the police officer, shaking Snipper by the paw. *"Þu talar ispiksu!"*

"I only speak a few words, I'm afraid," responded Snipper, reverting to Hedgelandish. "I do prefer to learn the language before I travel but I didn't know I was coming to Icepeak till yesterday."

"No problem!" said Ójafn, who spoke excellent Hedgelandish, like most Icepickers. "Not many hedgehogs try at all. Your pronunciation is anyway very good. So, follow me!"

When they emerged from the airport building, there was an icy wind blowing. Cold enough for winter in Hedgeland, thought Snipper. It was now, in fact, late May but he had come a long way north. Ójafn stopped in front of a sturdy-looking silver car.

"This is yours," he said. "It's a four-wheel drive so you don't have to stick to the made-up roads - though you should check first which routes are open. Most routes into the interior are impassable for another month. Do you intend to drive there at all?" Ójafn was

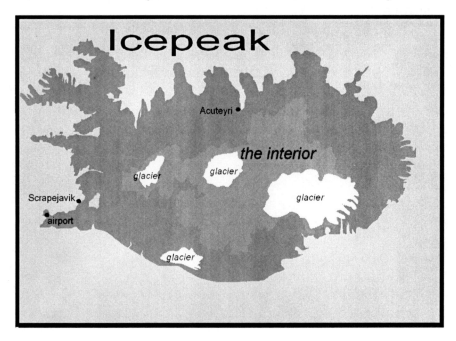

referring to the uninhabitable volcanic desert which occupied the centre of Icepeak.

"I really don't know yet," said Snipper, quite truthfully. In his job, he could rarely plan in advance where he was going - or keep to the plan if he did. "It's quite possible I will," he added.

"Well, if you're intending to drive through any rivers, you're waterproof up to here," said Ójafn, indicating a point halfway up the doors. "Always remember: point the car slightly downstream, drive slowly but never stop - the car may not start again if you do."

"Thanks, that's very helpful," said Snipper politely. He had, in fact, passed S.L.U.G's advanced driving test several years ago; but there was no need to say so.

"Good, well here's the key. The camping equipment, food and other supplies you asked for are in the back. You'll also find a distress beacon. I suggest you carry that with you at all times - it's about the size of a button, so you can slip it into the hem of your trousers. If you need help, just squeeze it for three seconds; it'll beam your location straight through to the Search and Rescue Association. After that it automatically transmits your co-ordinates at fifteen minute intervals, so don't press it again unless you want to cancel the call. Oh, and here's the reservation for your hotel in Scrapejavik. It's booked under your alias - that's correct, isn't it? Good. Well, I need to get back to the police station now so, if you're going directly to Scrapejavik, perhaps you could drop me off there?"

"Of course," said Snipper with a nod. He threw his bags into the back of the car and got into the driving seat, beside Ójafn.

Leaving the airport, they drove through a dull flat landscape strewn with mile upon mile of lichen-covered lava rock. Snipper had heard of Icepeak's great beauty, so it was a disappointing start. But the company was good, and Snipper soon discovered that Ójafn was a landscape painter, like himself. Ójafn assured Snipper there was plenty of outstanding scenery to paint in Icepeak; unfortunately, Snipper was equally sure there would be no time for painting.

Half an hour later, they were in Scrapejavik - a capital city in miniature with few grand buildings but lots of brightly coloured houses and wonderful sea views. After dropping his companion off, Snipper went and checked into his hotel. He then proceeded directly to Mr E's forwarding address: a freight company with its office close to the city harbour. The office in question was a small, low building with grey weather-boarding below and a blue corrugated-iron roof

above. Snipper climbed the short flight of steps to the front door. As there was no doorbell, he knocked.

*"Já!"* said a voice, inviting him inside.

Snipper let himself into a large bare room. Its one item of furniture was a desk. On the desk was a computer, a telephone and one neat pile of papers. At the desk sat a hedgehog with her nose in a book. Snipper decided that business must be slow today.

*"Godan daginn,"* said the hedgehog, looking up.

*"Godan daginn,"* responded Snipper, passing her a fake business card in his alias. "I wonder if you can help me. I own an outdoor leisure company in Hedgeland - we export a wide range of goods, such as walking boots, tents, portable stoves... Anyway, we're looking to expand into Icepeak, and we need to employ a local freight company. I'd like to enquire about your rates."

"I'm afraid, Mr Tennant-Pegg," said the other hedgehog, reading the name on Snipper's business card, "I don't think we'll be able to help you. We specialize in transporting bulkier items. But there's another freight company a little further down the street. I suggest you try them."

"All right, thank you, I will," said Snipper. He eyed the paper at the top of her pile, but it was only a repair bill for one of the company's lorries.

Turning to go, he opened the door to let himself out. It was a horrible windy day out there, and he paused on the threshold, apparently contemplating the weather for a moment before venturing out into it.

"The door! Please!" said the other hedgehog, shivering in her chair.

Snipper made as though to close the door, but not before a gust of wind blew into the room, scattering papers all over the floor.

"I'm so sorry - I should have been more careful," said Snipper. He shut the door firmly now but remained on the inside to help her gather up the papers.

"No, no, I can manage!" said the other hedgehog, not looking at all as though she wanted his help. In fact, when he saw how put out she was, he knew he was onto something.

"It's the least I can do," he insisted, stretching under the desk, where several official-looking documents had landed. He took a quick look at them and then went to collect some more papers which had blown right into the far corner of the room.

"Mr Tennant-Pegg!" said the other hedgehog, rushing to gather up the papers before he could get his paws on them. "These are private commercial documents. I really must ask you to leave."

"Oh, I see!" said Snipper, sounding slightly offended. "I assure you I was only trying to help - but, of course, I'll leave at once."

When she saw the wounded expression on his face, she looked a little embarrassed. However, he had seen enough by now. So he passed her the papers he was holding and left - closing the door behind him promptly this time. At the bottom of the steps, he glanced back to make sure she was not watching him through the window. Then he turned down the alleyway at the side of the office in search of the company's lorry park.

Here he hoped - and expected - to find several shipping containers. Several of the documents he had seen in the office had related to shipments from Hedgermany, where Gotha-Hölhog had his thermite factories. Snipper felt sure the thermite from those factories was now being shipped here. Icepeak was the last land mass before Gruntland, and Gruntland was certainly the final destination for the thermite. He wondered whether Icepeak was being used as an assembly point for whatever device would be used to disperse the thermite. He did not know what sort of device this would be, as thermite had never been used this way before. But he had noted with concern that the final shipment was due today. The plot, it seemed, was well advanced.

As Snipper had thought, at the back of the office was a yard parked with a small fleet of lorries. There were no hedgehogs in sight, so he got out his lock-picking equipment and a pawful of tiny tracking devices. Then, one by one, he undid the backs of the lorries, climbed inside and inspected their contents.

Three of the lorries were empty, but the others were all laden with crates. According to the labelling, two were carrying carbon steel casing and one was carrying operating systems. A fourth lorry was piled high with thermite. Snipper attached a tracking device to a crate in each of the lorries before relocking them. Then he returned to his car a couple of streets away and waited.

With time on his paws and not knowing when he would next get a chance to eat, Snipper decided to check the food supplies Ójafn had left him. A quick rootle revealed some rolls, sliced cheese and water. He made himself a sandwich and then settled down in the driver's seat to think about what he had just seen. The lorry load of thermite was no surprise, of course. The purpose of the other cargoes, however, was less obvious. Snipper wondered whether steel casing suggested some sort of pipeline was being constructed; but it was sure to have many other uses besides. As for operating

systems, these were the software that supported a computer's basic functions; but nowadays computers were used in almost everything - from factory assembly lines to washing machines...

A loud beep interrupted Snipper's train of thought. It came from his satnav: the first lorry was on the move. This satnav was naturally no ordinary run-of-the-mill satnav; it was a special-issue Secret Service gadget which displayed not only Snipper's location but also that of each tracking device. Currently, it was showing the first device (attached to a crate of steel casing) heading east out of Scrapejavik.

Snipper finished his sandwich and then had another look in the boot. This time he found a thermos flask containing coffee and some delicious yoghurt-covered raisins. After he had finished these, he settled down with a book called *Teach Yourself Icespeak* and waited patiently for the next beep. When it came, he checked his watch: it was precisely twenty minutes since the first lorry had set off. This time the cargo was the operating systems, but it was following the same route out of Scrapejavik as the first lorry. After another twenty minutes, he heard the third beep. Another lorry with carbon steel casing had set off in the same direction as the others.

Snipper had seen enough: it looked as though the lorries were all headed for the same destination. The purpose of the staggered departures was clearly to avoid the attention which a long convoy of lorries would have drawn. It was nearly time to pursue. He waited a further ten minutes, however, to give the lorry in front of him a head start. In the wide open spaces of Icepeak, it would be impossible to tail a vehicle from close behind without being spotted sooner or later; the satnav would allow him to follow from a safe distance.

When the ten minutes were up, Snipper started the car and headed east. Scrapejavik was a small city, so he was soon out of it and driving through flat grasslands. There were mountains in the distance but these were only faintly visible through the drizzle of rain which now descended. He glanced at the satnav. The lorry at the front of this little convoy had turned off the main road and was now heading south. The second and third lorries followed behind, carefully spaced at regular intervals along the same route. And now the fourth - and last - lorry was also on the move. Snipper's own car was halfway between the third and fourth and out of sight of both. Then suddenly the tracking device on the first lorry disappeared from the satnav's screen. Snipper tapped the screen with a claw but it made no difference. The device must have malfunctioned. There was nothing he could do, but it did not matter: there were two more devices ahead of him and they were both working.

The road now began to climb gently, and Snipper found himself skirting a large lake. Then Icepeak's rift valley came into view. This

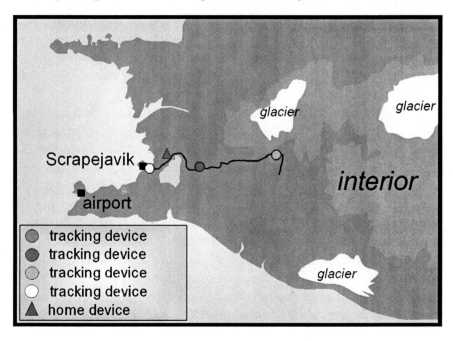

88

was where east and west were being pulled in opposite directions by the two great continental plates which lay beneath the country. Inside the rift the ground fell away abruptly, leaving a series of jagged land-locked cliffs at its edge. It was perhaps no surprise that, in ancient times, this dramatic place had been chosen as the site for the country's parliament - where the Icepickers had gathered to make their laws. Snipper glimpsed the view as he drove by and imagined these ancient hedgehogs making speeches from the cliff top. He would have liked to stop to get a better look, but there was no time. Instead he continued east, following the two remaining tracking devices on the lorries ahead of him.

Leaving the rift valley, Snipper continued into a rolling countryside of vivid green grasslands. Dotted here and there were low farmsteads, whose white walls and brightly painted roofs stood out stark in the treeless landscape. To his left could be seen, in the far distance, the edge of a massive glacier - one of the many which gave Icepeak its name. The weather was brightening now, and Snipper was beginning to appreciate the beauty of this unusual island. He wound down the window and breathed in the fresh air, which was scented with damp grass and a hint of wood smoke from a nearby farm.

Glancing at the satnav, Snipper now saw the second tracking device go dead in exactly the same location as the first. This was no malfunction after all. Had the devices been found and destroyed? He doubted it. The drivers were bound to be carrying mobile phones; so the discovery of one device would surely lead swiftly to the discovery of all the others. A more likely explanation was that the cargoes had been taken underground.

Snipper continued eastwards in pursuit of the one remaining tracking device ahead of him. As he was now expecting, after another twenty minutes that, too, disappeared. He carried on regardless, following the route the lorries had all taken.

Turning a corner, Snipper now caught sight of a plume of steam rising above the plains in the distance. He at once recognized this as Icepeak's world-famous geyser, a boiling-hot spring which every few minutes would erupt high into the air - creating a hundred foot column of scalding water. As he approached the place, there was a distinct smell of sulphur in the air; and he noticed that much of the hillside was covered in steaming pools bubbling with clear blue water.

The lorries had all taken their right turning just a short way past this extraordinary scene and then headed south. So Snipper turned right and headed south, too. When he finally reached the spot where the lorries had disappeared, he drove past it without pausing but took a good look as he went.

There was actually very little to see - a few glacial streams, an old turf-roofed house and more grass. Snipper parked some way on, along an old farm track which sloped downhill and out of sight of the road. He fetched his rucksack out of the boot, packed it with the necessary supplies and slipped Ójafn's tiny distress beacon into the hem of his trousers. Then he took a cross-country route back in the direction of the turf house.

As soon as the house came in sight, Snipper dropped to the ground. There was little cover to be had in this treeless landscape but at this distance the long grass would do. Taking his binoculars out, he scanned the scene. Naturally, there was no sign of the lorries; but he could see tyre tracks leading off the road towards the barn adjoining the house.

Turf houses were the traditional buildings of the island. While the fronts were made of wood, the roofs and sides were banked up with turf, to protect them against the harsh climate. In some cases, as here, the houses were built into the hillside to make them even more snug. But such buildings needed constant renewing and few survived; these days, when hedgehogs no longer lived paw-to-mouth, they preferred to live in modern homes with central heating.

All in all, it seemed an unlikely destination for the lorries with their sinister loads. First of all, it was too close to the road to be an assembly point for whatever Mr E and Gotha-Hölhog were assembling. Secondly, there was no infrastructure of any sort with which to assemble anything anyway. Snipper wondered for a moment whether it might be a halfway house – a place to store the cargoes before they were taken on somewhere else. Yet it looked scarcely big enough to store one lorry load - let alone three. Last but not least, these simple old houses had not been built with basements - so why had the signals from the tracking devices disappeared?

As the fourth lorry was now only a few minutes away, Snipper decided to watch and wait. Shifting in the long wet grass, he helped himself to an oat biscuit from his rucksack. Then he glanced at his watch - about three more minutes to go.

The lorry arrived bang on time and, sure enough, it came off the road and headed along the tracks to the turf house. The barn door, however, remained shut. Instead, much to Snipper's surprise, the entire front end of the barn opened out, allowing the lorry to drive inside. Ten minutes later, the lorry came out again and returned the way it had come - presumably minus its cargo.

It was time to have a look inside. Keeping low, Snipper approached the turf house from the side, where there were no doors or windows. When he got there, he paused to listen for voices or other noises to indicate hedgehogs within. There were none. So he crept round the corner and peered through the first window. Inside was an old-fashioned kitchen with an iron stove, a table laid for two and, in the middle of the table, a vase of fresh flowers. But there were no hedgehogs in sight, so he put on his gloves and, levering the window open with his penknife, slipped inside.

Once in, he made straight for the door, which was slightly ajar, and peered into the adjoining room. It was a sitting room - old-fashioned again but comfortably furnished. Three armchairs were arranged in a semicircle facing a blazing fire. In one of the chairs sat an elderly hedgehog in national dress. She appeared to be fast asleep. Above the mantelpiece hung old family photographs - one looked like the elderly hedgehog in her younger days. Snipper had to pinch himself. Had he stumbled into the home of some innocent Icepicker? Had he imagined the lorries and the connection to Mr E? The photographs, the table laid for two, the blazing fire and, above all, the hedgehog asleep in the chair suggested that he had; but he knew he had not.

Snipper tiptoed over to the door on the far side of the room - the door to the barn where the lorries had unloaded. It was locked. So he took out his lock pick and opened it as quietly as he could - only to be faced with another door. This one was made of metal and had neither lock nor handle. As he searched the room looking for some secret button or lever, the elderly hedgehog stirred. Snipper froze. Her eyes were still shut but she shifted in her chair, as though trying to make herself more comfortable. Then she gave a little sigh and seemed to lapse back into a deep sleep. Snipper resumed his search. He checked inside a cupboard and behind the pictures but then the rim of the mantelpiece caught his eye: at its centre was a carved flower, the middle of which looked as though it had been made separately and inserted as an after-thought. He pressed his paw against the flower, and the metal door opened - making a hissing sound as it did so. Snipper looked round in alarm, fearing the sleeping hedgehog must have been woken, but she slept on.

Snipper stepped into the pitch-black of the barn and pulled the two doors shut behind him, as gently as he could. Switching on his torch, he could just make out a modern, industrial-looking interior, equipped with what looked like pulleys, a forklift truck and a console with an array of buttons and levers. There was, of course, no sign of the cargo, and Snipper was now quite certain it was being

93

stored underground: somewhere in this room there was bound to be a trap door. He swept the walls with his torch looking for a light switch but found none. Stepping down the short flight of stairs leading into the room, he went over to the console and examined it. There was nothing that looked like an on-switch, so he ran his paw along the underside of the console; as he did so, he felt a small key-sized slit. He rummaged through his rucksack and pulled out a bunch of keys – copies of the ones in Mr E's hotel bedroom. Taking the slimmest, he inserted and then turned it; one by one, the ceiling lights came on.

The full extent of the room was now revealed, and Snipper gaped in astonishment. The original barn had clearly been extended right back into the hillside. Along its length ran a railway track, which then disappeared into a tunnel. Suddenly the turf house made sense. What better disguise for a tunnel entrance than a traditional Icepicker house built into the hillside? It also explained how so much cargo could be unloaded in such a small house and why the tracking devices had disappeared into thin air.

Snipper looked down at the console, whose display screen had lit up. It showed a small rectangular icon sitting on a double line. He guessed the rectangle must represent some sort of shuttle and the line was the railway track. Then he noticed, in the centre of the console, a panel of buttons and levers labelled "remote drive". Clearly it was possible to summon the shuttle. He stretched out his paw but, before he could decide which button to press, the little rectangle began to move of its own accord, slowly from left to right: someone was coming.

Snipper looked around but there was nowhere to hide. The only place he might have a chance of boarding the shuttle unseen was in the tunnel. So he walked over to the tunnel entrance and looked inside. On either side of the railway track was a narrow ledge - just wide enough for a hedgehog to stand on. Snipper went back to the console and, turning the key, returned the room to darkness. Then he made his way back to the tunnel with the aid of his torch. There he stepped up onto the right-hand ledge, walked along until he was out of sight of the tunnel entrance, switched off his torch and waited.

It was an awfully long wait and he began to wonder whether the shuttle was really coming. Every now and then, he glanced at his watch: ten minutes went by, then twenty and still nothing. But patience is one of a secret agent's most important qualities; and, eventually, after he had been waiting some twenty-five minutes, he thought he could make out the sound of a distant rumble coming from deep within the tunnel. Gradually, it got louder and louder. Then suddenly there was a burst of sound as the shuttle sped past him - missing him by a whisker.

A few seconds later, the noise changed pitch, indicating that the shuttle had emerged from the tunnel. Snipper heard the screech of brakes, followed by footsteps and voices. There were two hedgehogs and they were speaking Hedgelandish; one had the drawl of the southern United Stakes but the other sounded like a local.

"Well, that's the lot then," said the Icepicker. "All we have to do now is to stand guard, and that shouldn't be too difficult! After all, who is going to come looking here?" He chuckled. "Hey, I don't know about you, but I'm very hungry..."

"Gee, Nagli, so am I but you know we're all out of food. I guess we're gonna have to wait."

"Maybe not, Rollo. If I am very quiet, I should be able to find something from next door without waking the old hedgehog... You see, we're right on time for her afternoon nap!"

"Shall I come with you?" asked Rollo. Snipper thought he sounded reluctant.

"No, Rollo, you stay here and send the shuttle back. They'll want it parked at their end - in case they need to leave in a hurry."

"Sure thing, Nagli," said Rollo.

The sound of footsteps followed by a faint click indicated that Nagli had now disappeared into the turf house on his food-hunting mission.

"Darn it!" muttered Rollo to himself. "There's something wedged in the console... Well, ain't that weird? A brass button... but we ain't got no brass buttons on our clothes."

Snipper pricked up his ears in alarm. Feeling his jacket, he found that the top button was missing. But surely Nagli and Rollo were not the only hedgehogs to come through here? That loose button could belong to anyone! Would Rollo - who Snipper thought sounded none too bright - really guess there was an intruder in their midst?

"Oh, never mind!" said Rollo, who clearly had a bit of a habit of talking to himself. "Better get that shuttle outta here afore Nagli comes back and wonders what I've been doin'!"

So Snipper's presence remained undetected. Breathing a sigh of relief, he inwardly urged Rollo to do as he promised and send the shuttle back quickly before his more intelligent companion returned. Then he heard it - the noise of the shuttle's engine starting up and then gradually coming closer. This time it came towards him slowly - there had been no time for it to accelerate. Snipper flicked on his torch and jumped as it passed. He landed uncomfortably but safely inside the cabin. It was a small space, with just enough room for two hedgehogs. Snipper rearranged himself and then took a look behind: attached to the shuttle was a long trailer. This was no doubt designed for ferrying cargo, though currently it was empty. Behind the trailer was another cabin, enabling the shuttle to be driven in either direction.

Before long, the shuttle really began to gather speed. Snipper hurtled through the darkness for about thirty minutes before the shuttle started to slow down again. Now he had to think. He was anxious not to be spotted coming out of the tunnel. There could be no question, however, of jumping out onto the narrow ledge even at this speed. So he slid off the seat into the footwell and curled up as tightly as he could.

A few minutes later, the shuttle emerged into another industrial-looking space and came to a halt. This place seemed many times bigger than the barn in the turf house and was piled high with crates. It looked deserted but Snipper could see a CCTV camera pointed directly at the tunnel exit. Uncurling as little as possible, he reached inside his rucksack, pulled out an electrolaser gun and fired an electric current directly into the camera. There was a sizzling sound and a small puff of smoke: the camera was history.

Snipper stepped out of the shuttle and checked his satnav, but there was no signal. As he had suspected, he was still underground: that was why the tracking devices had appeared to vanish into thin air. He went over to the crates and examined them. As well as thermite, steel casing and operating systems, there were other crates containing rocket heads, guidance systems and fuel.

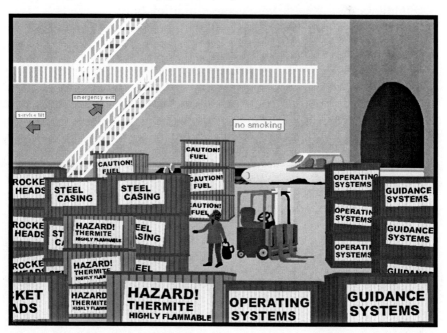

So that was it. Icepeak was not just an assembly point. Rocket heads and guidance systems meant missiles. Icepeak was to be the launch site. From here Mr E and Gotha-Hölhog would fire enough thermite-filled missiles at neighbouring Gruntland to melt one of the biggest expanses of ice in the world - drowning millions of hedgehogs in the process.

But why? What could be in it for them? Snipper thought back to Van Hogloot, whose home would be swept away if Mr E and Gotha-

Hölhog had their way. Then he remembered Mr E's hotel in Hogeveen. Hogeveen would narrowly escape the floods and become a coastal town. But even Mr E would not drown millions of hedgehogs just so that his measly little hotel could be by the seaside. Seaside hotels are neither that difficult to buy nor that profitable. There had to be some other reason, reflected Snipper. But there was no use dwelling on it now - not when he could be discovered at any moment.

First and foremost, Snipper needed to find out where he was. Ignoring the service lift, he took the stairs up to the emergency exit. As he pushed open the door, he paused, blinded by the sunlight. Since he had entered the turf house it had turned into a beautiful day - a complete transformation. Shielding his eyes with his paw, he stepped outside. Gradually, his eyes grew accustomed to the brightness; but what he saw made him blink hard.

In front of him lay a vast undulating desert of grey-black grit, stretching as far as the eye could see. The only relief from the interminable greyness was the odd patch of old snow left over from the winter. Snipper bent down and scooped up a pawful of the coarse grit: it was pumice, spewed out by one of the island's many volcanoes. Then he sniffed the air, but the place was barren and odourless: nothing could grow here. This was the interior, where no

hedgehogs lived and few travelled.

Snipper had another look at his satnav. He was about thirty miles north-east of the turf house. It was the perfect place for Mr E and Gotha-Hölhog to operate undisturbed. The nearest road was miles away; and in any case no hedgehogs would be travelling along it at this time of year. It would be late June before the road opened up for the few brave souls who dared venture this way - when all the snow and mud had finally gone. But snow and mud presented no problem for Mr E and Gotha-Hölhog: everything they needed could be transported through their secret tunnel.

Snipper decided to have a look round. The building he had just emerged from was a massive concrete construction. High atop its roof was a cluster of aerials and satellite dishes. Just round the corner from the emergency exit, he came across a second building, faced with corrugated iron. He noted that both buildings were entirely grey and blended well into the landscape. From the air they would be invisible to the casual observer.

However, there was no sign of a launch pad for the missiles. Snipper got out his binoculars and searched the vast and apparently empty landscape. Eventually, he spotted an ironwork look-out tower near the horizon. As he scanned down from it, three low circular structures came into view, which he recognized as underground missile silos. Surrounding the silos and the tower was a perimeter fence, which looked as though it was probably electrified. Mounted on the look-out tower were two infrared searchlights: their beams would be invisible to the naked eye and to any aircraft passing by; the searchlight operators, however, could view the infrared images on a special screen. At present, there were two hedgehogs keeping watch from the tower while two more patrolled the fence below; all of them were armed. Meanwhile several other hedgehogs wandered around the site with clipboards and appeared to be checking that everything was in order.

Snipper looked inside his rucksack: he had enough explosives to blow the missile silos sky-high. However, it was pointless trying to get to them while it was still light. Unfortunately, this being Icepeak in late May, it would not be dark until half past midnight. That meant he would have to wait ten hours. Anything could happen in ten hours. So he determined to do what he could in the meantime. Putting his binoculars away, he returned to the basement. Here there were no guards or any hedgehogs to be seen at all. So he decided he would destroy the guidance systems while they were still in their crates. Without those systems, the missiles were going nowhere.

When he had first arrived, Snipper had spotted a forklift truck. He now used this to unstack a pile of crates. Next, after a quick glance round to check he was still alone, he took a crowbar and the electrolaser gun out of his rucksack. He used the crowbar to lever open the lids and the electrolaser to fire an electric current into the contents, destroying them. Finally, he gathered up the loose nails, dropped them into his pocket and replaced the lids. He then paused briefly to glance round before getting to work on the next lot of crates. There was no one there. So he returned to the forklift truck and once more manoeuvred the forks under the uppermost crate and lowered it to the ground.

"Stop right dere," said a hedgehog with a strangely musical voice.

Snipper turned round in his seat. Three hedgehogs wearing traditional Icepicker jumpers were pointing guns at him. One of them - the one with the strangely musical voice - was none other than Despina.

Snipper stared, unable to believe his eyes. He tried to say something but the words would not come out. It felt as though someone had hit him in the pit of his stomach. This just did not make any sense. Following the avalanche, he had been sure of Despina's innocence. After all, she could have been killed; so how *could* she be on Mr E's side? She had even risked her life for the other hedgehogs on the train. And later - when they had all finally been able to holiday in peace - she had joined Snipper and his friends every day. Why? Much of the time it had just been the two of them but she had never tried to question him about his work. They had skied together and talked together; he had thought they understood each other.

Despina looked at him coldly. There was no friendship in her eyes. There was not even a flicker of recognition. "You will come down from de truck an' put your paws in de air," she ordered. Snipper did as he was told. "Now search 'im!"

One of Despina's hench-hogs picked up the crowbar and electrolaser gun. The other frisked Snipper but all he found were the nails from the crates. Snipper's rucksack lay just out of sight, behind the forklift truck.

"I found zese nails on 'im," said the hedgehog who had frisked him. He spoke with a Furzish accent, and it seemed to Snipper that, whatever Mr E's own nationality, he ran a very international outfit. "Ozzerwise 'e is clean."

"No, he isn't," said the other hedgehog, who sounded Bristlish. He had just stumbled upon the rucksack and was now examining the contents. "Take a look at this!"

"Le' me see," said Despina.

He showed her. She appeared to be impressed by what she saw and was about to take the rucksack from him; but he closed it and slung it back over his shoulder.

The search over, Snipper was pawcuffed and marched upstairs. They then led him down a long grey corridor past an array of hedgehogs with white coats and clipboards, deep in conversation. At the end of the corridor was a door guarded by another hedgehog, in what was clearly a uniform of Icepicker jumper and denim trousers. Despina knocked and then opened the door without waiting for a response. She motioned Snipper to go through and then followed him together with her two hench-hogs.

The room was a large wood-pannelled conference hall with a round table in the middle. Seated at the table were Mr E, Gotha-Hölhog and several other hedgehogs whose faces Snipper recognized from Secret Service files. There was Dr Prong from

Pawcelina, the owner of several construction companies; flouting planning and safety laws alike, he employed illegal slave labour to build on the cheap. Then there was Lieutenant Colonel Sharpshott, who ran a large private army out of the United Stakes: this army had been known to topple regimes and start civil wars all around the world; and it was not choosy over which side it fought for - so long as the money kept rolling in. Last but not least was Hejov-Darcnis, an arms dealer from Brusshia, who could lay his paws on anything from pistols to missile casing. It was a very international gathering, and all their names had appeared on the report about Van Hogloot.

"Come in, Mr Snipper," said Gotha-Hölhog, with the faintest trace of a Hedgerman accent. "We've been expecting you."

"You have?" said Snipper. He noticed a panel of TV screens on the wall opposite. One of them was blank, and no doubt its feed came from the camera Snipper had put out of business. However, there was another one showing the tunnel entrance from a different angle. He kicked himself for missing it - but cameras are not difficult to conceal.

"CCTV," explained Gotha-Hölhog. "You destroyed one of our cameras, I believe, but you clearly have no understanding of whom you are dealing with. We have cameras everywhere. We naturally have need of them to protect us against trespassers."

"Or the law," said Snipper pointedly.

"The law!" scoffed Gotha-Hölhog. "Such a middle class concept! Oh, I suppose it has its place - ordinary hedgehogs such as yourself need boundaries. But great minds must be free to operate as they see fit - what interest after all had Ilexplanter the Great in other hedgehogs' laws? You see, you have - in your rather inept and amateur way - stumbled upon a consortium of the greatest criminal minds in the world."

"Welcome," interjected Dr Prong, with a little bow of the head, "to headquarters of C.L.A.W. - Committee for Landscaping, Architecture and War."

"Ilexplanter the Great built an empire," said Snipper, ignoring Dr Prong. "What will *you* build by raising the sea level and drowning millions of hedgehogs?"

"A great deal," said Gotha-Hölhog. "The world will see a flowering of architecture greater than any before." He swivelled round in his chair and pointed a remote control at the wall. A huge screen descended from the ceiling. He pressed another button, and the screen lit up, showing a map of the world. "First we must wipe the slate clean. Ask yourself, how many of the beautiful coastlines of the world have been ruined by dull housing estates and hideous concrete towers? Take your own country, for example," he said,

zooming in on Great Bristlin. Getting up from his chair, he pointed at the south-east coast. "This coast was once beautiful. You had pretty towns and charming countryside but now the towns have been ruined and the countryside paved over. We shall sweep that all away."

He pressed another button, and the map changed again. The towns he objected to so much had now disappeared under the sea - along with vast swathes of eastern Hedgeland and much of the rest of Bristlin's coastline. In their place, there arose fresh developments dotted here and there along the new coastline. Snipper stared at the map, appalled by what he saw.

"We shall build new seaside towns," continued Gotha-Hölhog. "Beautiful towns which hedgehogs will *want* to live in. The land for this has been chosen very carefully, on the basis of a 7.2 metre rise in the sea level - the exact rise that will follow the melting of all the ice on Gruntland."

"So that's why you've been buying up land in northern Hedgermany?" said Snipper.

"Precisely," said Gotha-Hölhog. "And my colleagues here have also been buying - each in their own country. Dr Prong here has bought land in Pawcelina, Lieutenant Colonel Sharpshott in the United Stakes and Hejov-Darcnis in Brusshia. Last but not least is

Mr Lynchpin here" - Gotha-Hölhog indicated the hedgehog whom Snipper knew as Mr E. "Mr Lynchpin is in charge of the improvements in Great Bristlin."

Snipper frowned. So Mr E was calling himself Lynchpin now; and he Bristlish – or pretending to be. Somehow Snipper had expected that he would now finally learn what the E stood for, but perhaps he would never find out this hedgehog's real name. Looking at him, Snipper noticed he was no longer wearing his monogrammed cufflinks: he wondered whether the others knew he was Mr E. Then their eyes met. It sent a shiver down Snipper's spines. For all the others' evident disregard for life, there was something in Mr E's eyes yet more ruthless still.

"How d'you do, Mr Snipper," said Mr E. "Perhaps you would like to see the architects' drawings?" He took the remote control from Gotha-Hölhog and squeezed it in his paw. Drawings of a smart terraced street, a town square and a country hotel appeared on the screen. Snipper had to admit to himself it all looked very pleasant - but that was beside the point.

"What about the great architecture on the existing coastline?" challenged Snipper. "And historic buildings like Pawvensey Castle? What about Vertice - one of the most beautiful cities in the world?" He glanced at Despina but she did not react. It seemed too preposterous that she, who had been raising money to save Vertice from sinking into the sea, was now working with those who would consign it to the waves forever. Surely Van Hogloot was not more of a patriot than she. Perhaps, he thought desperately, this was all an act. Might she not be a spy working under cover against C.L.A.W.? But, if that was the case, why had she stopped him from destroying the guidance systems?

"What about all the hedgehogs," said Snipper finally, in a forlorn appeal to compassion, "who live and work and go to school along the existing coastline?"

"There will be casualties," said Mr E with a sigh, as though it troubled him a little, "but the path to greatness is not an easy one: sacrifices must be made."

"Hogwash!" said Snipper, bristling with anger now. "*You* are making no sacrifices. This isn't about great architecture. You're buying up land on the cheap - land which will double in value when it gets its sea view. You sneer at the middle classes but you're just a bunch of property developers!"

"Enough!" barked Mr E, banging the table with his paw. He turned to his colleagues: "We have indulged him long enough."

"Your plan will fail," put in Snipper quickly before they could take him away. "I've just destroyed half your guidance systems!"

"No, Mr Sneepper," sneered Hejov-Darcnis, who Snipper guessed must be in charge of the missile components; he spoke with a heavy Brusshian accent. "What you dyestroyed are *spyares*. We had already enough guidance seestems to assyemble meessiles and myelt all ice in Gruntland."

"I've destroyed your spares?" repeated Snipper, staring at Hejov-Darcnis and wondering if he was telling the truth. But what point would there be in lying at this stage? His heart sank. If he had only destroyed their spares, he had made no difference at all - he had not saved a single life.

"Take him away!"

It was Mr E who spoke now and he beckoned to the guards who had brought Snipper in. They came forward: one pressed his gun into Snipper's back, while the other used his to indicate the door. Snipper moved towards the exit but Despina was standing nearby and he paused in front of her, staring so hard she was forced to meet his gaze.

"Why?" he asked finally, his voice so weak only she could hear it.

Her eyes seemed to glisten in response, and he wondered for a moment if perhaps she really was on his side, but she did not speak.

"What's this?" said Mr E, stepping forward. "You know each other?"

Despina turned to face Mr E. Putting her paw on his arm, she smiled reassuringly: "We met on de train after de avalange, dat is all. Unfortunately, 'e did not introduce 'imself to me. If I 'ad known 'e was a spy," she continued, turning back to Snipper and looking him coldly in the eye, "I would 'ave killèd 'im."

Mr E watched them both, trying to read their expressions. Despina looked as though she had meant every word but Snipper knew she was lying. He wondered what Mr E would think if he knew they had not only met *before* the avalanche but had holidayed together *after* it. He also wondered what Despina would think if she knew that Mr E had started the avalanche which could so easily have killed her. Concentrating hard, Snipper wiped the emotion from his face. Whatever was going on between the two of them, he was not going to be the one to undeceive them about each other.

"I see," said Mr E, slowly. He looked at Despina suspiciously. "Well, you weren't to know he was a spy. Of course, now you do know and here he is... but perhaps we should finish this conversation in private."

He nodded to the guards, who pushed Snipper out of the room and marched him downstairs. Walking along between them, Snipper felt oddly disconnected from the threat of impending death. Somehow there seemed to be too much else to think about - such as the relationship between Mr E and Despina. She had lied to Mr E and kept Snipper's identity from him on the train. Mr E, for his part, had clearly been prepared to see her die in the avalanche he had started. Yet it also seemed to Snipper that there was an understanding between them - something more than just a working relationship. The way Despina had spoken to Mr E, placing her paw on his arm, had suggested warmth - intimacy even.

A beeping sound interrupted Snipper's thoughts. The guard in front of him paused to check his phone. "Change of plan," he said briefly. He then turned round and led Snipper and the other guard back the way they had come, until they reached the very exit which Snipper had taken when first getting his bearings at C.L.A.W. H.Q.. Going out through the door, they walked a little way from the building and then stopped. The two guards now both stood facing Snipper, guns to the ready, but silent and immobile. Snipper looked round but there was nothing to see - just the endless desert of black volcanic sand as before. It disturbed him. He had hoped C.L.A.W. would want to keep him for questioning or as a hostage; either would buy time. But, if they meant to lock him up or question him, why had they brought him out here? Suddenly, the awful truth dawned on him. They meant to kill him - *right now.* But he could not die now - not when the world needed him most. Unless he could stop C.L.A.W's evil plot, millions of hedgehogs would be drowned.

"What are you waiting for?" he asked quietly, suppressing the fear and turmoil he felt within.

"They are waiting for their orders, Mr Snipper," said Mr E, who just then emerged from the building with Despina. "You see, we've been discussing what to do with you - and who is to do it. Despina here regrets very much that she didn't kill you on the train and is anxious not to let slip a second opportunity. And I, for one, cannot bear to disappoint her."

He nodded at Despina, who turned to face Snipper and drew her gun. For a brief moment, her paw trembled. Snipper stared at her. Was that fear he saw in her eyes? No, the look - whatever it had been - was gone. There was nothing now - neither fear nor pity... nor any sign of feeling at all. Very slowly she raised the gun so it was pointing directly at him, and at last he realized she was for real. She had no heart - all that had seemed good in her had been a lie. He had to think - and think quickly.

"You're making a big mistake..." he said, racking his brains. "I have... I have a tracking device implanted in my arm. Kill me and it'll send a signal to Secret Service H.Q.. They'll be here before you can launch a single missile."

Mr E raised his paw, motioning Despina to stop. "Then we will have to remove it."

"It's tamper-proof," said Snipper quickly. "If you remove it, *that* will alert Secret Service H.Q., and they'll come after you just the same."

"Really! What a convenient story!" said Mr E disbelievingly. He hesitated nevertheless and was clearly weighing up the situation. Could he afford to take the risk? After all, if the Bristlish Secret Service turned up now, it would all be over for C.L.A.W.. "Well, congratulations!" he said sarcastically. "You've exchanged a quick death for a long and lingering one." He now turned to speak to his two thugs. "Guards! You are to escort Mr Snipper on a journey. I'm afraid he may prove to be a somewhat troublesome passenger. I suggest you put him out for the duration."

Mr E's two hench-hogs approached Snipper menacingly. He frowned instinctively, as though about to curl up into a ball to protect himself; but it was impossible with his arms pinned behind his back. He braced himself for the blow...

## Chapter Three

When Snipper came to, every bone in his body seemed to ache, and a cold wind ruffled the fur on his stomach. He shivered and opened his eyes; above him was the open sky and all around was an empty desert of grey-black sand. There was no sign of C.L.A.W. H.Q. and not a hedgehog in sight. He had been dumped in the middle of the wilderness.

Shivering again, he sat up; his jacket, shirt, watch and shoes had all been taken from him. Mr E had been clever. Dumping Snipper in the desert meant a lingering but certain death. Out here, without any water supply, a hedgehog might be expected to survive for three days at most. Long before that, however, cold and lack of shelter would cause hypothermia to set in, rendering a hedgehog helpless. Mr E must have calculated that, by the time Snipper died and his death set off the device in his arm, it would be too late for the Secret Service to stop the missiles.

As it happened, there was no device in Snipper's arm. He had invented the story to save his life. He did have Ójafn's distress beacon hidden in the hem of his trousers, but this was a perfectly ordinary little device. Had Mr E known where to look, he could easily have removed it without alerting anyone.

Snipper was tempted to use the distress beacon, but the Search and Rescue Association was not equipped to deal with the likes of C.L.A.W., and he would have to think this through carefully. Remembering the map on his satnav, he guessed that C.L.A.W. would have dropped him roughly to the north-east of their H.Q., as this would leave him further into the interior and further away from help. If so, C.L.A.W. would lie beneath the flight path of any helicopter coming to his rescue from Scrapejavik; and C.L.A.W. would not hesitate to shoot it down. If only he could speak to the rescue party and get them to put him through to Ójafn! But this tiny distress beacon was no communications device; it would send his position and a summons for help, and that was all. It was its simplicity that enabled it to be so small and light – and so easy to hide.

Snipper left the beacon where it was: he would use it only as a last resort. Sitting on his haunches, he now examined the landscape around him. The prevailing winds in Icepeak he knew to be easterly, while the shape of the dunes ahead suggested the wind blew to his left. That meant he must be facing north. Above him, rain clouds blotted out the sky, but there was enough of a faint glow to betray the sun's position. He estimated therefore that it must now be about six or seven o'clock in the evening. That meant he had about six hours of daylight left. Once night came, his core body temperature would start to drop dramatically. Memory loss would probably follow, together with confusion and drowsiness. The one certainty, if he stayed here, was eventual death.

Getting to his feet, Snipper searched for vehicle tracks but there were none. They must have dropped him by helicopter. He made for the nearest hill to get a better view but there were no landmarks or features of any kind. In the absence of any other clues, he decided to head south-west. If he was lucky, he might stumble across C.L.A.W. H.Q.. Failing that, he would eventually have to hit farmland - if he could survive that long.

He started to walk. It was hard; he was shoeless and the ground beneath him shifted with every step; but he was driven on by the thought of the millions of hedgehogs whose lives now rested in his paws. He walked step after step, hour after hour until dusk fell. Time was running out. He climbed to the top of a ridge and again surveyed the scene before him. As he looked, his heart sank, and he slumped onto his knees. Before him stretched more of the same - an interminable desert of black grit.

It was no use carrying on. There was no way he was walking out of here before nightfall. Shivering with cold, Snipper tore open his trouser hem and extracted Ójafn's distress beacon. For a second or two, he stared at the device in his paw, hesitating. If he activated the beacon, would the rescue helicopter be shot down by C.L.A.W. before it could get to him? Or was there *any* chance they might delay sending out a rescue party while they contacted the police? It was Ójafn's beacon, after all, and he was a police officer...

Snipper feared the worst; but it was not only his own life that hung in the balance, and he could no longer see any alternative. He squeezed the beacon for three seconds, as Ójafn had instructed. Its tiny red light then began to flash on and off, and he put the beacon away in his pocket. As he did so, the weather took a sudden turn for the worse, and torrential rain began to pour down from the heavens. He lay down, curled up in a ball and embraced the cold. In the distance, a gap had opened up in the clouds and the moon's ghostly rays cast a small pool of light on the dark sand. It was beautiful, in a strangely hostile sort of way. Snipper allowed himself one last look. Then he closed his eyes and focussed on his heart beat. Gradually it slowed. His breaths became fewer and shallower, and he felt himself

being sucked down into a deep dark well. Now his heartbeat was a faint and intermittent quiver. He was scarcely breathing. The heat drifted from his body but the shivering had stopped. Then finally the darkness enveloped him, and he slipped from consciousness.

Chapter Four

Despina knelt down by Snipper's body and held her paw against his neck. He was deathly cold. She paused, searching for a pulse, however faint, but could feel nothing. Then, shining her torch over his chest, she suddenly noticed how still he was. He was not breathing at all.

She was too late. The tears welled up inside her. She tried to keep them back - tried to think clearly - but it was no good. Until now she had suppressed her feelings but this was too much. She sobbed violently, her hot tears falling on Snipper's face. She blamed herself. She had been too concerned to preserve her own cover. If only she had acted sooner, Snipper might still be alive.

Now she had lost him, and the fate of millions of hedgehogs rested in her paws alone. It was sheer madness to pit an amateur like herself, with just two weeks' training, against the might of an organization such as C.L.A.W.. She remembered how her government had first approached her - had told her it was a simple job, just a matter of passing information. Then somehow the job had snowballed, sweeping her along with it.

She pulled herself together. How could she be so spineless? She might be an amateur but no one had seen through her cover yet - not even poor Snipper. She kissed his cold, lifeless face goodbye and got to her feet. She had to focus now. Though as yet she had no clear plan, there was still just enough time to stop Lynchpin and the others. Wiping the tears away, she felt the old steely determination come back. She turned towards the car and made to go. Then something made her stop in her tracks. She pricked up her ears. There had been a tiny sound of something moving behind her. She swivelled round and shone her torch on Snipper. He was breathing! She dropped to her knees and held her paw against his chest. His heart was beating again, and the warmth was flooding back into his body.

"Snipper!" she gasped.

Snipper opened his eyes and blinked in the glare of her torch. She pointed it away from him so he could see who it was. He blinked again - this time with astonishment and distrust. He had been expecting a rescue party - not *her*. He lunged at her but she drew a gun from her jacket before he could grab her.

"You!" he snarled.

"You're alive!" exclaimed Despina.

"Do I disappoint you?" he asked bitterly, staring down the barrel of her gun.

"No!" protested Despina. "I 'ave come to rescue you."

"Rescue me!" snorted Snipper. "So why are you pointing a gun at me? And, if you remember, you're the one who seized me in the first place. You're the one who would have killed me back at C.L.A.W. H.Q.."

"No!" protested Despina. "No, I would *not* 'ave killèd you. I 'ad to pretend-a because dey were watching. I 'opèd someting would 'appen... dat you would do or say someting - and you did - but, if I would 'ave to shoot anybody, it would *not* 'ave been you."

"No one's watching now, though, are they?" responded Snipper, between gritted teeth. "And what are you doing in Icepeak anyway, if you're so innocent? Nobody forced you to come here and do their dirty work for them. And nobody forced you to produce those maps showing them where their wretched new coastline would be. When we were in Itchaly, I thought you were my friend; but you were just using me - trying to find out what I knew."

"Using you?" retorted Despina, suddenly bristling with anger. "*You* were de one dat follow *me*! I did my best to discourage but you would no' take de - 'ow you say?"

"The hint?" suggested Snipper, sniffily.

116

"Yes, de 'int!"

"I didn't notice much discouragement in Clawtina!" said Snipper.

"No," admitted Despina, self-consciously. "You wore-a me down."

"I wore you down?" murmured Snipper, taken aback by her explanation. He hesitated. "You're telling me it was real - our friendship?"

"Yes," said Despina. "For me at least, it was real."

Snipper looked at her, unsure whether to believe her or not; but, if she was his enemy, then why had she come out here? Why had she not just left him to die?

Despina sighed: "Look, what is your alternative? I leave you 'ere or you trust-a me!"

Snipper reflected a moment longer. There was no sign of a rescue party, and time was running out. "All right," he said. "You may have a point but, if you want me to trust you, you can start by putting that gun away."

Despina did as he asked, and the two hedgehogs headed over to her car. As they walked, Snipper put his paw in his pocket and took out Ójafn's distress beacon. For a moment or two, he watched its tiny red light as it flashed intermittently. Then he squeezed the device for three seconds, until the red light finally stopped: the summons for help was cancelled.

"That's *my* car!" exclaimed Snipper, as they drew near. "How on earth did that get here?"

"I found it in de basement at C.L.A.W. H.Q. and brought it up in de service lift."

"I see," said Snipper. He realized C.L.A.W. would hardly want to leave his car parked outside the turf house. Had the Secret Service come looking for him, the car would have shown them the way. "Weren't you spotted?"

"Yes, one of de guards saw me, but I jus' told 'im dat I was following Lynchapin's orders."

The two hedgehogs climbed into the car. Snipper noticed, attached to the dashboard, his own special-issue satnav. Despina switched it on, and immediately two tracking devices started to flash their position on the screen.

"What's this?" he asked, pointing at the satnav. "Have they brought the crates out of the basement?"

"No," frowned Despina, not understanding. She was not aware that he had attached devices to the crates. "I found some tracking devices in your rucksack," she explained. "I 'id one at C.L.A.W. H.Q. and one on de 'elicopter which took you away. Dat was 'ow I found you. Of course, when I got to de place indicated by de tracking device, you were gone but I saw your footsteps in de sand and I follow. Sometimes de tracks disappearèd wi' de wind but I saw you were 'eading sout'-west, so I drove on until finally I found you."

"Where's the rucksack?" asked Snipper. He spoke in a business-like manner and showed no sign of appreciation for what Despina had done.

"On de back seat, wid your clo'es," she said, trying to sound as business-like as possible, herself.

Snipper turned round. "That's not mine!" he exclaimed with bitter disappointment.

"No, it is mine but de contents are yours. When de guards took you away in de 'elicopter, dey gave me your rucksack. Lynchapin told me to put it in 'is office. So I did. First, 'owever, I moved your tings into my own rucksack."

Snipper picked up Despina's rucksack and checked the contents. The majority of his things were there - most crucially the explosives, detonators and timers. He was also pleased to see his night-vision binoculars, can of insulating foam, bolt cutters, duplicate keys and gun, all of which might be required tonight. A couple of items were missing, however, and he still could not quite shake off his suspicions about Despina.

"What about my lock-picking equipment?" he demanded. "And the other binoculars? There were two pairs..."

"I could not fit everyting in," said Despina defensively. She had been surprised by just how much Snipper had been able to get inside his rucksack. Years of practice, as he travelled the world on secret missions, had made him an expert in efficient packing. "Also I could not find de clo'es you were wearing before, but de clo'es from your rucksack are on de back seat."

Snipper made no further objections. He picked up the clothes which Despina had rescued – the black clothes he packed for nocturnal operations – and dressed in silence.

"What's this?" he asked, picking up a folded piece of paper he found nestling inside his fleece.

"It is a map of de missile silos. I stole it from Lynchapin's office."

Snipper unfolded the piece of paper and examined the map. He could scarcely believe his eyes: it showed the exact position not only of the missile silos but also of the entire underground complex beneath them. Finally, he began to relax a little. It seemed to him now that Despina *had* to be telling the truth. If so, she really was the most amazing hedgehog he had ever known. Not only had she got most of his equipment back, she had found the map, taken possession of his car and then tracked him down in the middle of nowhere. The admiration he had felt for her before, in Itchaly, was as nothing to what he felt now; with the map, his bag of tricks and Despina on his side, he suddenly felt in control of the situation again.

"So, I too 'ave a question," said Despina, turning down the heat now that he was dressed. "When I found you, your 'eart did not beat and you were cold like ice... You were dead. Now you are alive." She looked at him almost accusingly.

"I wasn't dead. I was hibernating."

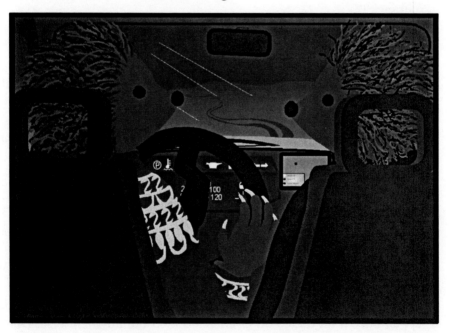

" 'ibernating?" repeated Despina, who did not understand the term.

"Yes, I was practising the ancient art of hibernation. It's when you make your body slow down to preserve energy."

Despina had never heard of such a thing. She looked at him wide-eyed: "Is it dangerous?"

"Not usually; it just takes a lot of practice and focus. In prehistoric days, when hedgehogs were hunter gatherers, we all used to hibernate to get through the winter. It meant you could survive in very low temperatures and with no food - though you need to put on a good deal of weight first to survive for any significant period of time. Of course, modern hedgehogs don't need to do it and have mostly forgotten how. Historians will tell you it's a lost art but there are still a few of us who know how to do it."

"You mean it is part of de Secret-a Service trainin'?"

"Secret Service?" murmured Snipper, as though he were surprised by the suggestion. He knew she must have worked it out by now; yet somehow it still went against the grain to admit it.

"Yes, Snipper," said Despina, looking him straight in the eye. "Of course I know you are a secret agent. Why else would you 'ave come to dis place? Why else would you carry explosives in your rucksack?"

"Mm, I suppose you have a point," he confessed. "It's just I've never told anyone before - not even my family."

"Dat mus' be very lonely."

"Yes, it is - but the same must go for you. I mean, all that stuff about working for W.I.S.C.A. was just cover presumably?"

Despina shook her head. "No, I really do work for W.I.S.C.A.. I am not like you - I am not a professional spy. I am an 'ydrologist: my job is to research de rising water level which menace Vertice. But one day Lynchapin callèd me on de telephone. 'E gave 'is name as Pungolo and say 'e was environmentalist 'oo want some maps showing de effect of a 7.2 metre rise in de sea. I 'ad never 'eard of 'is company, so I look on de internet and whadda do I find? Dere *is* no such company. So I go straight to de *polizzia*."

"Why straight to the police?" asked Snipper. "I mean, he was obviously dishonest but it isn't a crime to lie - thank goodness."

"No, but I ask myself: why de precise 7.2 metre rise? Dat would 'appen only if all de ice on Gruntaland melt but nowhere else. Dis is not possible. Such maps may be interesting but dey are not useful. Yet I could tell e' want dem very much indeed - too much."

"I see," said Snipper, "you've obviously got a nose for trouble."

"Per'aps," said Despina, with a shrug of the shoulders. "Anyway, de next day I was visited by an 'edge'og from S.N.A.I.L. - de

*Servizio Navale Avanscoperta e Indagini Litorali.* S.N.A.I.L. is de coastal reconnaissance and investigations service of our navy. It is responsible for de security of Itchaly's coastline. But per'aps you already know dis?"

Snipper nodded: he had, indeed, come across S.N.A.I.L. before. "So they told you to play along, did they? But why all the cloak and dagger stuff in Vertice and on the train?"

"In Vertice?" repeated Despina. "You were dere?"

"Yes, that's actually when I first saw you. I was in a restaurant with my friends when I heard you busking in the piazza. It was so beautiful, Pawline and I went outside to listen. Then I noticed a hedgehog from the audience taking an envelope out of the collection box and tucking it into his sleeve. I had no idea what I'd stumbled across at the time but I guessed something was up. Then, later on - once I'd realized who he was and seen you with him on the train, I was sure you were working together. I imagine the envelope contained the arrangements for you to meet on the train?"

"Dat's right," said Despina. "S.N.A.I.L. told me to say to Pungolo dat I knew 'e was not for real. I tell 'im de *polizzia* 'ave been asking questions and we 'ave to meet secretly. Dey wanted 'im to tink I could be bought."

"Good idea," said Snipper. "That's often the first step towards building trust with a criminal. But something must have gone wrong. I mean, you do know that he started that avalanche? He very nearly killed you! Though clearly you patched things up pretty well between the two of you later on..."

"Patchèd tings up?" repeated Despina, looking perplexed.

"I saw you put your paw on his arm in C.L.A.W. H.Q. - and the way you looked at each other. It didn't seem like a mere business arrangement to me."

"I see..." said Despina, who now looked a little embarrassed. "Well, 'is attitude changèd. At first, 'e trust-a me but dat was all. I was replaceable and 'e was not caring if I live or die. Den, of course, I survivèd de avalange and 'e was not knowing dat I sospect 'im for it. So S.N.A.I.L. sent me to Icepeak and told-a me to make myself indispensable dis time. My instructions were to make 'im tink I care for 'im..."

"You're a good actress," murmured Snipper pointedly.

"And you are not a good actor?" retorted Despina, needled by his critical tone. "You - a spy - you never lie?"

Snipper thought of all the aliases he had assumed over the years (of which Hobjay-Dart and Tennant-Pegg were only two) and of the countless lies he had told. But he had never been called upon to pretend to care for someone whom he really disliked. The very idea was horrid to him, and he was not even sure he could do it. He ought, of course, to consider himself lucky that he had never needed to. He should admire, not criticize, Despina. Her mission could hardly have been more important and, if ever the end justified the means, this was it.

"I'm sorry, that wasn't fair; and you're quite right, I've told plenty of lies in my time. You're immensely brave to do all this and follow him to Icepeak. What I don't understand, though, is how you convinced him to let you come here in the first place - before you won him over, so to speak."

"It was simple. I contact 'im again an' say I am going to Gruntaland to do some research. I ask if 'e want any more information, and 'e say yes. 'E want me to make a map which show de varying dept' of de ice across Gruntaland."

"So C.L.A.W. could target their missiles to best effect?"

"Exactly. Of course, I did not give to 'im de correct information. I also invented several 'ot spots under de ice."

"Hot spots? Like under a volcano?"

"Dat's right. Dere is one in Gruntaland, and some scientist tink dere may be more. Anyway, I put several on de map... where dey were least likely to be."

"Hm, I think I see..." said Snipper, thinking it through. "I suppose the point is that, if the ice above a hot spot melts, it releases a volcanic eruption?"

"Yes, and den de lava from de 'ot spot spread out an' melt de surrounding ice, too. Which mean jus' one missile could melt an area for which normally you would need two or maybe more... Now C.L.A.W. tink dey know where dere are 'ot spots all over Gruntaland, but dey are wrong."

"So, if the worst comes to the worst and we can't stop them," said Snipper – and, as he spoke, a little shiver ran down his spines - "at least they won't fire enough missiles to melt the *whole* of Gruntland."

Despina nodded. "So, anyway," she said, "you askèd 'ow I came to Icepeak. Well, after I 'ad spent several weeks in Gruntaland, I came 'ere to deliver my map an' my explanations to Lynchapin. Once 'ere, I... well, I workèd on getting to know 'im..."

"OK," said Snipper, "but you're a scientist - why did they send you after me with those two thugs?"

"Dat was my idea. Dey trust-a me by now, and de guards are not so clever, so I volunteer. I tought, if I could get de chance to be alone wid you, I could explain everyting and, you and I, we could join forces."

"So they were never suspicious of you?"

"Not til after you arrivèd. I 'ad never told dem about you. Dey only guess 'oo you are 'cause dey know an agent callèd Snipper is on de tail. Den, when Lynchapin saw de way you look at me, I 'ad to admit dat we 'ad met on de train. Dat was why Lynchapin wanted *me* to kill you. It was a test."

"I'm sorry," said Snipper. "I really put my foot in it, didn't I? Thank goodness you seem to have a pretty good survival instinct! ...So what were you planning to do next?"

"Well, I *was* trying to discover de identity of de leader. But no one 'as ever seen 'im - 'e never come to Icepeak. All communication wid 'im is by telephone or by email, and everyone jus' call 'im Mr E. Even Lynchapin, 'oo is responsible for de liaison, 'as never met 'im. So, unfortunately, de identity of Mr E is a mystery."

As she spoke, Snipper stared at her in astonishment - not because she had failed to identify Mr E and Lynchpin as one and the same. Rather he stared because, with her Itchalian accent, she pronounced his name with the stress on the "Mr" and not on the "E". The way *she* spoke it, it came out as "mystery"! It was a play on words! Perhaps the letter E was not his initial after all. Perhaps Lynchpin *was* his real name.

"You're wrong," he said. "You've met Mr E but you just don't know it."

Despina frowned at Snipper: she clearly had no idea what he was talking about.

"*Lynchpin* is Mr E."

"Lynchapin!" exclaimed Despina. "But e' takes 'is orders from Mr E!"

"He may pretend to," said Snipper.

"But why?"

"Perhaps he doesn't trust the others... or he may plan to double-cross them - after all, we know he's completely ruthless."

They lapsed into silence for a while, as Despina negotiated her way around a large stretch of snow and mud. It seemed extraordinary that she had managed to drive to his rescue all the way out here - at a time of year when most of the roads through the interior would still be closed. But Snipper was beginning to understand that she was no ordinary hedgehog.

"Unfortunately," said Despina, once they were clear, "dere are more important tings to worry about now: C.L.A.W. 'ave brought forward de firing of de missiles. Before I drove 'ere, I radioed to my H.Q. and told dem everyting. Dey 'ave contacted your service and also de Icepicker police... but I understand de defence of Icepeak, it is de responsibility of de United Stakes?"

Snipper nodded. "That's right – Icepeak's too small to have its own army. So, what were your instructions?"

"De United Stakes army is now standing by to attack. S.L.U.G. and S.N.A.I.L. will assist but dey say dat *we* mus' try first."

"They're right," said Snipper. "An open military assault could easily fail. It's certainly no use trying to bomb the silos. Being underground, they're practically bomb-proof. The silo covers might be damaged but that wouldn't delay the launch for long. No, we need to get inside them and it's easier to do that covertly. Do you know how long we have?"

"Until six in de mornin'."

"I see," said Snipper, checking the satnav: C.L.A.W. H.Q. was very close now but it was already well past midnight and it would be dawn in less than three hours. "I had feared they might bring it all forward. Since I turned up, they're probably worried the authorities are onto them; and, now that you've disappeared, they'll know you're a spy, too."

Despina dipped the headlights now and slowed right down to reduce the noise of the engine. Finally, as the ground began to rise and there was a risk of being seen, she stopped the car and turned off the lights. Snipper fished around in the rucksack and pulled out a two-way radio.

"You'd better stay in the car," he said, passing her the radio. "If I don't return within two hours, call for help. The radio's set to the correct frequency. You just have to press this button here."

"I'm not staying in de car!" said Despina, bristling with indignation. "You 'ave a saying, I tink: 'many paws-a make light work.'"

"It's dangerous, Despina! You're not a professional. I'm paid to take risks."

"I 'ave 'ad de secret agent training," she protested.

"OK..." said Snipper hesitantly. He wondered just how thorough any training could have been, given the short time she had been with S.N.A.I.L.. His own training had lasted months, and he had four years of practical experience behind him. "What did they teach you?"

"Radio communications," she said, "shootin' an' paw-to-paw combat. For two weeks, when I was supposèd to be in Gruntaland, I was actually at de S.N.A.I.L. *Academia*."

"I see," he said. Sabotage was the skill they were most in need of now. However, she had already shown how very resourceful and capable she was - it seemed she could turn her paw to anything she chose. "All right, then," he said, relenting. "I'll show you what to do, and then we'll have to go straight away. It'll be getting light again soon, and we've got just five hours and twenty-three minutes before they launch those missiles!"

Snipper now swapped his jeans for a pair of black trousers, to complete the black outfit he wore for all nocturnal operations. Then the two hedgehogs left the car and headed up the ridge which separated them from C.L.A.W. H.Q.. As they neared the top, they dropped to their knees and crept forward. Snipper took out his night-vision binoculars and searched for the launch site.

As before, there were two guards patrolling the perimeter and two on the look-out tower. Otherwise, the site was empty. The perimeter guards, with only the moon and low-intensity torches to light their way, would be able to see ten feet ahead at best. On the tower, however, they were now using their infrared searchlights to sweep the area. This would be tricky. Though Snipper was able to see the beams through his night-vision binoculars, they were invisible to the naked eye. For much of the operation, Snipper and Despina would have to rely on precise timings to avoid stepping into the searchlights.

Snipper now rummaged about in the rucksack and took out the bomb-making equipment and an extra fold-away rucksack. He then gave Despina a quick demonstration, showing her how to lay the explosive, how to wire it to the detonator and timer and how to set the timer. Once he was sure she knew exactly what to do, he divided the equipment between them.

The two hedgehogs then picked up their rucksacks and crept down the hill until they were within a few yards of the perimeter fence. Here they paused, while Snipper watched the patrolling pattern of the two guards through his binoculars. They took a total of eight minutes to complete a circuit, and the spot where they passed each other was outside the reach of the searchlights. This, therefore, was where Snipper and Despina would break in.

"Ready?" whispered Snipper, as he watched the guards approach each other. "We go... now!"

They rushed forwards to the fence. As Snipper had suspected, it was electrified. He sprayed the wires with foam insulation and cut through them with fibre-glass-handled bolt-cutters. He then pushed the wires outwards, creating a hedgehog-sized hole in the fence. "I'll go first," he whispered, anxious to make sure it was safe. "Then you throw the bags through and follow."

They were through with two minutes to spare. Snipper pulled the fence back into place. They now headed towards the base of the tower, where they would be shielded from the searchlights. Once there, Snipper re-examined Despina's map of the launch site. Then he picked up his night-vision binoculars once more and watched the sweep of the infrared beams. The searchlights took five minutes to cover an arc of approximately 200 feet; the nearest and furthest silos were both in full darkness for ten minutes - the middle silo for just five.

"Right, this is the plan," he whispered. "You can take the nearest silo. We'll go there together and, once I know you're safely in, I'll

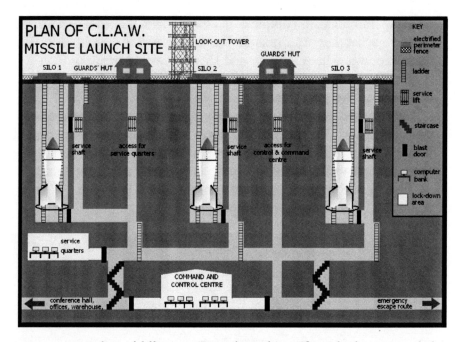

PLAN OF C.L.A.W.
MISSILE LAUNCH SITE

LOOK-OUT TOWER

GUARDS' HUT

SILO 1    GUARDS' HUT    SILO 2    SILO 3

KEY

electrified
perimeter
fence

ladder

service
lift

staircase

blast
door

computer
bank

lock-down
area

service
shaft

access for
service quarters

service
shaft

access for
control & command
centre

service
shaft

service
quarters

COMMAND AND
CONTROL CENTRE

conference hall,
offices, warehouse,

emergency
escape route

move on to the middle one. Lay three lots of explosive around the missile and set the timer for twenty past two. Remember to check the time before you come out. That's essential: otherwise you could step into the searchlight and you won't even know it - not until the shooting starts, anyway. So. The searchlight takes seventy seconds to pass over the silo and there are ten minute intervals between sweeps. That means you'll need to exit between one and eleven minutes past two. Got that? Good. I suggest we synchronize watches. Mine's coming up to one thirty-nine. When I say 'now', set your own to that time... OK?... now!"

"What about de last silo?" asked Despina, as she pressed the button on her watch.

"I'll do that one as well," said Snipper. "I'll be closer to it anyway. When you've finished, return here and we'll leave together."

"What if someting goes wrong?"

"Then I'm afraid it's every hedgehog for him or herself."

Despina nodded, and Snipper picked up his night-vision binoculars again.

"OK," he said, as he watched the infrared beam move from one silo to another, "We'll go on the count of five. One, two, three, four... five!"

The two hedgehogs reached the first silo just as the searchlight left it. Alongside the main opening was the service hatch, but there

128

was a lock on it. Breathing deeply so as to stay calm, Snipper felt the shape of the keyhole with his paw. Then he selected a key from his bunch of duplicates. It fitted. He pulled the hatch open, waited for Despina to climb in and then closed it behind her. With three minutes to spare, he moved on swiftly to the next silo, unlocked it, slipped inside and pulled the hatch down just as the searchlight swept over.

Inside was a short ladder leading to a cage lift. Snipper got into the lift and examined its three buttons - they were marked *Exit, Upper Missile Chamber,* and *Lower Missile Chamber and Command Centre.* He pressed the second button. The lift jerked into action and, after a short descent, came to a halt again. In front of him was a reinforced-steel blast door, which separated the service shaft from the missile chamber. He turned the wheel on the door anti-clockwise, pushed it open and stepped out onto a narrow walkway. Below him was a drop of at least a hundred feet and, rising up through the chamber, a missile of immense proportions.

There were four ladders running down the length of the chamber. About halfway down was a second walkway, connecting to four steel arms which clamped the missile into place. Snipper climbed down to the lower walkway and then up one of the steel arms so that he was right up close to the missile. He checked his watch - he had

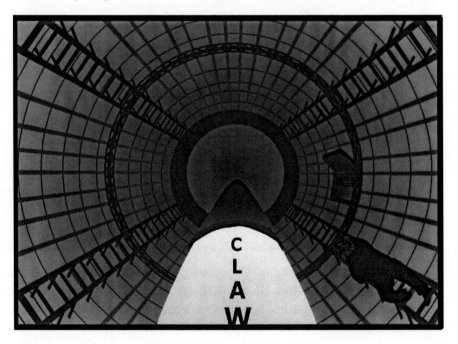

given himself just nine minutes to lay the explosives. Working quickly, therefore, he assembled the first device and attached it to the missile with a magnetized holder. He set the timer for twenty past two.

It was now eleven minutes to two. He was still on schedule. So he stepped out onto the thick metal rib which ringed the missile and made his way carefully around it. He then attached two further devices at even intervals and climbed back up to the service shaft.

As he exited the lift, he checked his watch again. The searchlight would be directly overhead for another four seconds: he waited six for good measure. Then he pushed open the hatch, climbed out and crept over to the third silo.

He was able to move faster this time, for the silos were all identical. As before, he took the lift down one level, went through the blast door, and climbed down the ladder and out towards the missile. He attached the first device, then stepped out along the rib ringing the missile and attached the second. As he was assembling the third, he heard a sound above him.

Someone had just entered the missile chamber. Working as fast as he could, Snipper attached the last device, while trying not to be distracted by the sound of footsteps coming down the ladder. As the enemy hedgehog reached the steel arm which Snipper himself had come along, Snipper was just setting the timer. He turned, and suddenly they were staring at each other.

The enemy hedgehog raised his gun. Snipper swiftly ducked. A bullet smacked into the missile casing just inches from the bomb and then ricocheted off round the chamber. Snipper now moved as fast as he dared round the missile's narrow ledge - focussing his eyes away from the death drop below. More shots rang out. This time one of the bullets grazed his leg. Just a few steps further and he would be out of the line of fire. Ignoring the pain in his leg, he pushed on to the next steel arm and then just beyond...

He had made it. For the next few seconds, at least, he would be safe. He looked at his watch: it was fourteen minutes past two.

"There are three bombs attached to that missile!" he shouted. "You've got just six minutes to get out of here!"

For a moment there was silence. Then there were more footsteps. Snipper got out his gun and returned to the steel arm he had just passed. The enemy hedgehog was back on the walkway which circled the chamber and coming towards him. Snipper fired off a warning shot and then threw himself down onto the steel arm, just as the enemy hedgehog opened fire again. Snipper now half slid, half crawled, down the arm. As he did so, a bullet caught the edge of his paw, and his gun fell clattering to the floor of the chamber. He was

now defenceless. More to the point, there was little he could do to stop the enemy hedgehog from trying to defuse or remove the bombs – if he had the stomach for it.

"That's five minutes now!" shouted Snipper between gritted teeth.

The enemy hedgehog immediately fired off two more rounds as though to prove something, but then the shooting stopped. Snipper looked round to see him retreating back up the way he had come. No doubt he intended to warn C.L.A.W. but he would certainly be too late. Breathing a tiny sigh of relief, Snipper wrapped a handkerchief round his paw. Then he stepped out onto the adjoining ladder. A stab of pain shot through his injured leg as he did so, but he took no notice and climbed down to the base of the missile chamber as quickly as he could. He retrieved his gun from the floor and hurried over to the lower blast door. But now a loud scraping sound above made him stop in his tracks. He looked up: the silo cover was moving back. Then a siren sounded, followed by an announcement over loudspeakers.

"Action stations! Action stations! All hedgehogs to their stations. We are under air attack. Stand by to launch missiles."

So the United Stakes Army had decided they could wait no longer: but they had chosen the worst possible moment to turn up. Despina was up there, waiting for him, about to find herself in the middle of a pitched battle; and there was nothing he could do about it. To make matters worse, C.L.A.W. had reacted by deciding to launch their missiles right away. It was already too late, of course; the missiles would be blown up before they could leave the silos. But, with the covers open, the force of those explosions would wreak havoc above ground. Surely Despina would now abandon any idea of waiting for him; but what if she were trapped by the fighting, unable to flee? She had said S.L.U.G. and S.N.A.I.L. would assist if the United Stakes Army attacked: so, right now, S.N.A.I.L., at least, should be looking for her. But in the half-dark, amid the chaos and confusion, there was no guarantee they would find her.

Snipper looked at his watch: it was seventeen minutes past two. Grasping the wheel of the blast door in both paws, he tried to turn it, but it was stuck. He tried again but it was still no good. A shiver of fear ran down his spines. What should he do? If he went back up, he would be shot as soon as he left the silo. If he stayed where he was, he would be killed by the explosion. He paused for a moment, trying to think. Overhead, there was a buzzing sound. So the army

helicopters had already arrived! For a moment, the missile chamber was flooded in a dazzling white light as their searchlights swept the compound. Then came an exchange of gunfire: the battle had begun. Summoning every last scrap of strength, Snipper heaved at the door one last time.

It opened! Panting with the effort, he almost fell through the door and then pulled it back behind him. But now it would not shut. He tried again and again but it really was no good. There were now just two minutes left before the explosion - and, with all that fuel on board, it was going to be a big one. Looking around, he saw that he was now at the bottom of the service shaft, but straight ahead was a ladder leading down into the heart of the underground complex. Abandoning the door, he practically tumbled down the ladder.

Now finding himself in a long corridor with a staircase just ahead, Snipper took the stairs. He half ran, half stumbled down them. At the bottom he turned left, down another longer corridor - neither knowing nor caring where it led: he was running for his life. The adrenalin killed the pain in his leg, and he ran faster than he had ever run before.

Then it happened. There was a huge bang and, a fraction of a second later, the force of the explosion thrust upwards and outwards. A ball of flames burst out of the silo's opening, lighting up the night sky, as the thermite burned with intense ferocity. At the base of the

silo, an eruption of hot gases and debris swept through the open blast door, down past the ladder, along the corridor and down again.

Snipper threw himself to the floor and curled up in a ball, as it swept towards him. A moment later it was upon him, forcing him to

cover his eyes with his paws, enveloping him with its searing heat and choking the breath from his body. Seconds passed like hours... but, eventually, the gas and the heat dispersed.

It was over. Coughing and spluttering, Snipper got to his feet and brushed off the soot. The pain had returned to his leg and the fur on his paws was singed; but, considering what could have been, he reckoned he was doing pretty well. What about Despina, though, up there all on her own, abandoned by him? Snipper wanted to go and find her but there was no going back the way he had come. After an explosion of that magnitude, the service lift would be nothing more than a heap of red-hot twisted metal. As for the ladders in the missile chamber, they would have been blown to oblivion.

Checking the map from Lynchpin's office, Snipper noted that he was now at the very lowest level of the underground complex. Behind him was the way to the Command and Control Centre - where the criminal masterminds of C.L.A.W. were no doubt bristling with fury, as their plans lay in tatters. Ahead, however, lay the Emergency Escape Route and this was where Snipper now headed.

The Emergency Escape Route was another underground railway track, similar to the one which had brought him here from the turf house. This one, however, had a double track and a shuttle ready and waiting. Snipper boarded the shuttle, took it a short way into the tunnel, then stopped again and got out. Taking the necessary equipment from his rucksack, he assembled a small bomb and laid it on the track. No one else would be using the Emergency Escape Route after Snipper. For, though the bomb was small, it was big enough to destroy the tunnel entrance.

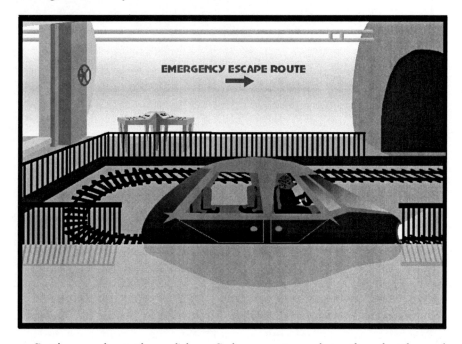

Setting a short time delay, Snipper returned to the shuttle and pulled the lever down hard. He moved slowly at first and then gradually accelerated until he was shooting down the tunnel at enormous speed. Hurtling through the darkness, he heard a distant rumble as the tunnel entrance collapsed; and for a moment he thought he glimpsed lights ahead - but this was probably just the reflection of his own headlights. He wondered where this tunnel would take him. Perhaps to the turf house? But that seemed an unlikely destination for an emergency escape route. Wherever it went, the main thing was to get back above ground. Then at least he could call Despina and find out if she was all right.

About twenty minutes later, the shuttle slowed and Snipper emerged from the dark tunnel into another windowless room. Unlike at the turf house, there were no steps here - just a ladder leading to a trap door. Parking behind a second, empty shuttle, Snipper disembarked and climbed the ladder. Opening the trap door a fraction, he felt a breeze ruffle the fur on his face. He sniffed and

136

smelt grass. Clearly he was no longer in the barren wilderness of Icepeak's interior; but there was no sign of life anyway - neither voices nor footsteps. He climbed out and waited a minute while his eyes acclimatized. Then he checked his watch: it was just after three o'clock in the morning. To his left, the sky glowed red. It was dawn. Then a glint of silver caught his eye: just a few feet away, lying in the grass, was a metal object. He went over and picked it up. It was a pewter hip flask. Turning it over, he saw there was an inscription.

*To our darling Scratch from Mum and Dad.*

Suddenly Snipper remembered the conversation with Scratch back in Vertice, on the first night of that fateful holiday. Scratch had lamented the loss of his hip flask while on exercise in Icepeak. What an extraordinary coincidence that Snipper should find it now! Then he remembered the photograph Scratch had shown them - the one with the strange ironwork tower in the background. He had thought it odd at the time. Now he realized it had to have been the look-out tower in the missile compound! If only he had realized it then...

Still, this was no time for reminiscing. Snipper tucked the hip flask into his jacket pocket, took out his satnav and checked his location. He was about ten miles north-east of the turf house - right next to Gatafoss and exactly where Scratch thought he had lost the flask. In a few hours' time, this spot would be busy with tourists visiting Icepeak's most famous waterfall. Snipper reckoned it was not a bad choice for an escape route: there was a road here, a car park and by day a hedgehog on the run could melt into the crowd – not generally an easy thing to do in this sparsely populated country.

Snipper also noted that he was about twenty miles to the south-west of C.L.A.W. H.Q.. As he turned to look that way, it suddenly dawned on him that the red glow in the sky was not the rising sun but C.L.A.W. H.Q. burning! Judging by the intensity of the glow, it looked as though the whole place must now be on fire. He hastily got his phone out and checked it for messages. There were two from Despina - one sent at two fifteen and the other at two twenty-five. *Where are you?* read the first message, *Am waiting for you beneath the tower.* Snipper scrolled down to the second message. *All 3 silos destroyed,* it read, *WHERE ARE YOU?* The second message had been sent more than half an hour ago. There were no more after that

- and now C.L.A.W. H.Q. was engulfed in flames. Fighting a rising sense of panic, Snipper dialled Despina's number.

" 'Allo?" said a strangely musical voice down the other end of the phone.

"Despina, it's me - Snipper!" he said breathlessly, as the relief surged through him. "Are you all right?"

"Yes - and you?" asked Despina nervously.

"Yes, I'm fine. I'm at Gatafoss. Where are you?"

"I am safe," said Despina. "A S.L.U.G. agent rescue me and now I am wid my colleagues from S.N.A.I.L. All de leaders of C.L.A.W. 'ave been caught - all except for Lynchapin. 'E trigger a lock-down, so de rest of dem were trappèd in de Command an' Control Centre -"

"*All* of them?" repeated Snipper.

"Yes. Lynchapin double-cross dem like you said 'e might. 'E 'ad made 'em sign a contract which say, if any of dem are caught, deir property will all go to Mr E. Dey never knew dat Lynchapin *was* Mr E."

"But how did he get away?"

"I don't know. I suppose 'e must 'ave used de Emergency Escape Route."

"The Emergency Escape Route?" repeated Snipper, frowning. "But that's not possible..." He was quite sure no one could have got through after him. Then suddenly he remembered the lights he had glimpsed in the tunnel and the second shuttle parked in the underground room – just feet from where he stood now. Mr E had been *ahead* of him!

The sound of an engine revving interrupted Snipper's thoughts. He looked up to see a motorbike coming straight for him. The rider was none other than Mr E. Snipper reached for his gun but Mr E already had his gun in his paw. He fired once... twice. The first bullet hit Snipper in the leg. The second got him in the chest. He fell to the ground, gasping for air. As he stared up at the dawn sky, a red mist descended over his eyes. Then darkness... and nothing.

## Chapter Five

Drifting in and out of consciousness, Snipper became vaguely aware that he was tucked up in bed. He had no idea where exactly but it was warm and cosy; and, tired as he was, that was all that seemed to matter.

Confusing images flashed through Snipper's head - a turf house, an avalanche, a hedgehog in blue and a vast moon-like landscape... There had been a dream – the maddest of dreams. Gradually, bits of it started to come back to him. In it he had been some sort of secret agent. And, although the thought of himself as a secret agent seemed absurd and even frightening, the parts of the dream he could remember had been vivid and full of excitement. He wondered whether his job as an art dealer was making him restless; it was interesting, certainly, but in a dry, intellectual sort of way. It would have been nice if, every now and then, there could have been a little more action in his life.

"Good to see you in the land of the living," said a faint voice from somewhere far away.

Snipper frowned. Propping himself up on his elbows, he surveyed his surroundings. Round him were three other beds, all occupied by hedgehogs with injuries of one kind or another. Standing at the foot of his own bed were two more hedgehogs, who seemed to have nothing wrong with them at all; they were even smiling at him. One wore a green coat and the other a thick woolly jumper; both looked strangely familiar, and yet he could not pin either of them down.

"Who?... What?" he murmured woozily.

"It's us - Pierce and Ójafn," said the hedgehog in the green coat. Snipper seemed to remember there had been a hedgehog called Pierce in his dream; he, too, had worn a green coat. "You seem a little confused," continued Pierce. "I expect the effect of the anaesthetic hasn't worn off yet."

"Anaesthetic?" repeated Snipper stupidly.

"Yes, you're in hospital, and they've been operating on you. You were shot - twice, I think, though you've got a couple of nasty grazes, too. One of the bullets got you in the leg but the doctors have removed it now."

"I see," said Snipper slowly, though he did not really see at all. He wondered why anyone would want to shoot an art dealer.

"The second bullet," said Pierce, "should have killed you but for this. We found it in your breast pocket." He produced a hip flask and threw it for Snipper to catch. "I don't know how you're going to explain that bullet-shaped dent to your friend."

Snipper pawed the flask, which had landed on the bed beside him. On it was an inscription: *To our darling Scratch from Mum and Dad.* Snipper remembered his friend Scratch saying he had lost his flask in Icepeak; but, if so, how had it come into Snipper's possession? He had never been there.

"I've never been to Icepeak," said Snipper, as though the others would have followed this train of thought.

"You're in Icepeak now," said the hedgehog in the woolly jumper, "in Scrapejavik Hospital. I'm Ójafn, the Icepicker police officer who met you at the airport."

Snipper gaped at Ójafn and Pierce, as it gradually dawned on him that he had not been dreaming at all. Indeed, when he thought about it, turf houses and moon-like landscapes fitted very well with what he had read about Icepeak.

"So, I really am..." began Snipper. Hesitating for a moment, he looked around at the other beds to check that none of the other patients was listening. Then, dropping his voice to a whisper, he said: "I *really am* a secret agent?"

"One of the best," said Pierce quietly. "You've just succeeded in foiling what was probably the most terrible plot in hedgehog history."

Snipper reflected for a moment. "I think there were some missile silos..." he said hesitantly. "Were there?"

"Destroyed - all of them. You did a very thorough job."

Snipper laid his head back on his pillow and stared up at the ceiling while the truth sank in. At first he felt awestruck by what he had been told and then elation. For it was all coming back to him now: how C.L.A.W. had plotted to raise the sea level by melting all the ice on Gruntland; how C.L.A.W. had hoped to profit by building new towns and villages to line the new coastlines; how he, Snipper, had tailed Mr E all the way to the middle of Icepeak, destroyed C.L.A.W's missile silos and escaped through an underground tunnel. Thereafter, though, it all became a blur again. He certainly had no memory of being shot.

"Who shot me?" he asked.

"Lynchpin," said Ójafn. "He was the only member of C.L.A.W. to get away and we found his motorbike abandoned at a small airfield just a few kilometres from where we found you. We ran some checks on that motorbike. It's registered to an elderly hedgehog called Broddóttir. She lives in a turf house about fifty kilometres north-west of C.L.A.W. H.Q.."

"You mean *the* turf house?" said Snipper. "The one hiding the entrance to the tunnel?"

"That's the one."

"Of course!" exclaimed Snipper. "When I went there, there was an elderly hedgehog asleep in the armchair. It seemed very strange. I remember being worried I might wake her."

"They were obviously hoping to put off any intruders," said Pierce. "Thank goodness it didn't work with you."

"I visited the turf house this morning," said Ójafn, "and had quite an interesting chat with Broddóttir. It turns out that her sister married a hedgehog from Bristlin and went to live there. The nephew from this marriage usually flies over to visit once a year or so. But recently he's become a frequent visitor and his stays have been lengthy."

"We'll let you guess his name," interjected Pierce.

Snipper frowned. He still felt far from clear-headed; but, after a moment's reflection, the penny finally dropped.

"Of course," he said at last. "Lynchpin!" As he spoke his name, the memory of their final meeting at Gatafoss at last came back to him. Lying back against his pillow, he saw in his mind's eye the moment the motorbike had borne down on him. He remembered the pain of the first bullet hitting his leg and how he had gasped for air at the impact of the second. He remembered falling to the ground and his phone slipping from his paw... his phone.. Had he been talking to someone at the time?

"Despina!" he exclaimed, fully alert at last. "Where's Despina?"

"I am 'ere."

Snipper looked round and saw a hedgehog in a pale blue dressing gown walking slowly towards him. Her arm was in a sling.

"You're hurt!" he exclaimed.

"It is notting - just a scratch," said Despina, with a dismissive wave of her paw.

Snipper thought she looked tired. "Come and sit down," he said. He waited for her to come round and take the seat by his bed. "Now tell me what happened."

"Well, I was waiting for you under de look-out tower, as you told-a me to. I was waiting since a quarter of an 'our when de missile silos open and I realizèd dat, if I stay, I would be killèd when de bombs explode. So I ran back to de 'ole in de fence where we come in, but I must 'ave run into de searchlight because someone shouted and fired. Dat was when I was injured; but it was just a scratch and a moment later de 'elicopters of de United Stakes Army arrivèd, so C.L.A.W. were no longer shooting at *me*. So now I wait outside de compound. By now all de missile silos were destroyed but dere was still no sign of you. I was wonderin' if I should go back to look for you... Den Pierce turn up and told-a me to leave wid 'im -"

"I can tell you she took quite a bit of persuading," interjected Pierce. "Naturally, I explained I was a S.L.U.G. agent and knew her from the train. But, when I told her there was a helicopter waiting to winch her to safety, she was very reluctant to leave without you."

"But Despina," said Snipper reproachfully, "I thought we'd agreed that, if something went wrong, it was every hedgehog for him or herself."

"But I *did* go wid Pierce," retorted Despina.

"Eventually - when the United Stakes Army started bombing the place!" said Pierce.

"You're lucky to be alive," said Snipper.

"As are you!" said she.

"Yes," replied Snipper quietly. "The difference is I'm paid to risk my life and trained for it. You're not. You've had a couple of weeks' instruction, of course, but a S.L.U.G. agent's training lasts six months. And, even then, we're expected to have several years' experience before going on a mission like this." Snipper paused for a moment, tired from the effort of speaking, but then resumed: "What I'm trying to say is that *that's* what makes your part in this mission so extraordinary and special. I know I couldn't have destroyed those missile silos without you. In fact, without you, I would have died in the wilderness before I'd even had a chance to try."

"The world will be forever in debt to both of you," said Ójafn.

"It certainly will," agreed Pierce. "Just think - out there, there are millions of hedgehogs going about their daily business right now as though today were just a day like any other... but who are, in fact, only alive thanks to the two of you. You know, Despina, you should think seriously about staying on permanently at S.N.A.I.L.. They'd have to be mad not to snap you up."

"Stay on?" repeated Despina, and it was clear the possibility had never even crossed her mind. "Abandon my job at W.I.S.C.A.? No, not while Vertice is still at risk. C.L.A.W's plot 'as been defeated, certainly, and Vertice is not abou' to disappear under de sea; but de risk of floodin' 'as not gone away. Already - you mus' know - we suffer terribly when dere is much rain or a stormy sea. It is still very urgent dat we find a way to protect our city before more damage is done - and, until we succeed, I stay."

"Well, Snipper, you - " started Pierce, turning to address his colleague; but Snipper had fallen asleep. "Sorry, Despina, you'll have to excuse him. He's lost a lot of blood and I think he's still under the influence of the anaesthetic. We probably ought to leave him to sleep it off."

"We should," agreed Ójafn. "In any case, you have a flight to catch, and I ought to get back to the police station - but I can give you a lift to the airport first."

"Well, it looks as though it's goodbye then," said Pierce, turning to Despina. He took her paw in his own and squeezed it.

"Goodbye, Pierce," said Despina, embracing him in the Itchalian manner. "Tank you for savin' my life. Goodbye, Ójafn."

Pierce and Ójafn now departed, and Despina was left on her own with Snipper. Sitting silently in her chair, she watched him as he lay asleep, his chest gently rising and falling with his breathing. She noticed that, every now and then, his whiskers twitched and, every so often, he tossed and turned as though he were having a bad dream. Perhaps he was dreaming about his job again. She wondered if she ought to wake him... but no, he needed sleep more than anything. Never mind if he was dreaming about the mission. She would leave him be and let sleeping hedgehogs spy.

## *The End*

# Post-Script: Geographical and Scientific Notes on "Let Sleeping Hedgehogs Spy"

The world inhabited by Snipper and his companions is in many respects very like our own, so you may be interested in the following facts.

## Italy: Venice

Much like Despina's home city (Vertice), the city of Venice is famed for its beautiful architecture and setting. Built on 118 small islands within a lagoon, it seems to rise from the sea, and the only way to get around is on water or on foot. Fortunately, it has over 150 canals and 400 bridges!

Venice's annual carnival, which is of medieval origin, takes place over the eleven days before Ash Wednesday. Balls, concerts, plays and shows are held; and everyone wears masks and fancy dress costumes. In the past, masks sometimes enabled people to get away with some very bad behaviour; this prompted the introduction of various laws, including one forbidding masqueraders from carrying weapons! These days people are much better behaved.

However, all is not well in Venice, which was built on marshland and has been sinking at a rate of about 10cm / 4 inches a century throughout its history[1]. The city is constantly threatened by floods, and a project is currently underway to construct mobile flood barriers at the lagoon inlets.

## The Italian Dolomites

From Venice you can take a train into the Dolomites, a spectacularly beautiful section of the Alps, with its jagged peaks of bare rock. Here you will find Italy's most chic ski resort, Cortina d'Ampezzo - a dead ringer for Clawtina!

---

[1] This figure comes from a study by UNESCO (the United Nations Educational, Scientific and Cultural Organization). UNESCO is a similar organization to Despina's WISCA, and has an office in Venice, which studies Venice's problems and possible solutions.

# Avalanches and Crevasses

Avalanches occur naturally, triggered by stress in or on the snow pack. This can be caused by heavy snowfalls, rising temperatures, rock falls, human activity or even the slow downhill creep of the snow pack. Avalanches can be tiny but the worst are hugely destructive. To avert any danger to people, minor avalanches are routinely triggered with explosives when no one is around.

Crevasses are deep cracks within glaciers and ice sheets. They are caused by varying rates of flow, such as when a glacier moves round a bend and the ice on the inside edge moves more slowly than that on the outside. They often have vertical walls, and can be up to 45m deep, 20m wide and several hundred metres long (148 feet deep, 65 feet wide and several hundred yards long). Sometimes they are hidden by overlying snow.

# The Netherlands

The Netherlands[2] is a low-lying country very similar to Van Hogloot's Needlelands. Much of its land is reclaimed from the sea. Excess water is pumped off this land and into canals. Before electricity, windmills provided the power to do this. Today, more than a quarter of the Netherlands is below sea-level - and these areas are home to about 3.5 million people.

# Iceland

Iceland is an island state, just like Icepeak. It forms part of the mid-Atlantic ridge caused by the tectonic plates[3] of North America and Eurasia pulling apart. As they pull, lava rises up from the sea floor and solidifies, widening the island by about 2cm / ¾ inch each year. At Thingvellir (ancient site of Iceland's parliament), high inland cliffs show clearly where the land has been pulled apart. Elsewhere the rift is marked by volcanoes and geysers (hot springs).

---

[2] The Netherlands are often referred to simply as "Holland". However, Holland is strictly speaking just one region of the Netherlands.

[3] Tectonic plates are a kind of skin around our planet. There are eight major ones and they float on top of molten rock.

The interior of Iceland is mostly an uninhabitable desert of grey-black grit. It can only be crossed in high summer when free from snow, floods and mud. However, the rain then flows into the ground too quickly for plants to grow.

Situated close to the Arctic Circle, Iceland has very long summer and very short winter days. Mid-summer's day lasts 21 hours 12 minutes.

## Greenland

Greenland, which is very similar to Gruntland, lies north-west of Iceland. It is both the largest island that is not a continent and the least densely populated country in the world. About 80% of it is covered in ice. Scientists believe that, if all the ice on Greenland were to melt, the sea level would rise by 7.2 metres / 24 feet.

## Hedgehogs

The hedgehogs in our world are much less highly evolved than Snipper and his companions, but they share the same roots and some characteristics. An excellent book on all things hedgehog-related is *The New Hedgehog Book* by Pat Morris.[4]

One of the most distinctive features of hedgehogs is hibernation. Along with dormice and bats, they are the only native British species to do this. Hibernation is often thought of as a kind of deep sleep but it is much more complex than this. The purpose of sleep is rest and recuperation, which is essential to survival. The purpose of hibernation is to conserve energy, and the need for this depends upon exterior conditions. In winter, when food supplies are low, a hedgehog risks expending more energy looking for food than he (or she) gains from eating. So he allows his temperature to fall from about 35°C to between 10°C and 1°C (95°F to between 50°F and 34°F) to save energy. This means other functions also have to slow down. Breathing almost comes to a standstill – with up to an hour between short bursts of breathing; and the heart rate slows to fewer than 20 beats per minute.

The duration of hibernation depends upon the climate. In Britain, hedgehogs usually hibernate from about November to March; but a

---

[4] *The New Hedgehog Book* by Pat Morris is published by Whittet Books.

warmer winter allows them to remain active well into December. Hibernation is never continuous. Hedgehogs can go for up to four months without stirring but usually wake up about once a week.

Although hibernation conserves about 90% of a hedgehog's energy, he must prepare by fattening up. This supports the remaining bodily activity and allows him to generate heat when the time comes to wake up.

## Night Vision

Despite being nocturnal animals, hedgehogs actually see less well at night than by day, like humans. There are, however, a number of night vision devices (NVDs) which can help us see in the dark. Some NVDs (like the searchlights at the missile compound) project a near-infrared beam to illuminate the landscape. This illumination is invisible to the naked eye but is converted into a visible image viewed through the NVD. Other types of NVD (like Snipper's binoculars) magnify the light naturally present and convert it into an image. The disadvantage of the first kind of NVD is that the beam can be seen by anyone else who also has an NVD.

## Thermite

Thermite is an iron oxide and aluminium powder used mostly for welding or cutting through metals. It has also been used in hand grenades, incendiary devices and for destroying enemy artillery. However, it is not an explosive so would not normally be an obvious choice for filling a rocket-head. C.L.A.W. chose thermite because it contains its own supply of oxygen and thus, once lit, cannot easily be put out. Thermite burns underwater, melts ice and reaches temperatures of up to 2,500° C / 4,500° F.

Fortunately, our world is on a somewhat bigger scale than Snipper's. As such, there is simply too much ice in Greenland to melt it all by artificial means. So we humans can sleep soundly in our beds in the knowledge that a plot such as C.L.A.W's would not work on our planet!

# Also by Elizabeth Morley

# Where Hedgehogs Dare

*Where Hedgehogs Dare* turns back the clock to the time of Snipper's great-grandmother, Snippette, and the beginning of the Second World War. Great Bristlin stands alone against Hegemony and needs every hedgehog it can get: Spike has joined His Majesty's Air Force and is flying reconnaissance missions; and Clou has formed an escape line to help Bristlish prisoners-of-war on the run.

Snippette is now determined to escape from her enemy-occupied island and do her bit for the war, too – even if it's just making widgets in a factory. However, the mysterious Field Liaison and Espionage Agency (known to its agents as F.L.E.A.) has something altogether more dangerous in mind, and Snippette will soon hold the fate of nations in her paws.

*..."Are you afraid to die?" asked the brigadier suddenly.*
*Snippette thought for a moment. "Yes, sir."*
*"Then what the blazes makes you think you could work for an organization like F.L.E.A.?"*
*"Some things are more important than my fear of dying."...*

*Where Hedgehogs Dare* takes Snippette, Flight Lieutenant Spike and Clou, the Comte de Grif, on a dangerous journey through enemy-occupied territory – a parachute drop, crash landing, secret messages, deception and self-sacrifice. Some will be captured. All risk their lives.

*...Spike swerved away from the oncoming planes but then others appeared, as if from nowhere. Suddenly they were on his tail...*

*..."They know what Clou gets up to... if they do capture him, he'll be shot."...*

Lightning Source UK Ltd.
Milton Keynes UK
UKOW05f1012031213

222277UK00003B/202/P